THE TRUMPETER
OF KRAKOW

THE
TRUMPETER
OF KRAKOW

ERIC P. KELLY

COLLIER BOOKS
Macmillan Publishing Company
New York

Macmillan Publishing Company
866 Third Avenue, New York, N.Y. 10022
Collier Macmillan Canada, Inc.

Library of Congress catalog card number: 66-16712

The Trumpeter of Krakow is also published in an
illustrated hardcover edition by Macmillan Publishing Company.
First Collier Books Edition 1973
10 9 8

Printed in the United States of America

ISBN 0-02-044150-9

To
Edward Lowell Kelly
Louville Howard Merrill

Contents

ANCIENT OATH OF THE KRAKOW TRUMPETER

"I swear on my honor as a Pole, as a servant of the King of the Polish people, that I will faithfully and unto the death, if there be need, sound upon the trumpet the Heynal in honor of Our Lady each hour in the tower of the church which bears Her Name."

THE TRUMPETER
OF KRAKOW

The Broken Note

It was in the spring of the year 1241 that rumors began to travel along the highroad from Kiev in the land of Rus that the Tartars of the East were again upon the march. Men trembled when they heard that news and mothers held their children close to their breasts, for the name "Tartar" was one that froze folks' blood in their veins. As the weeks went on, the rumors grew thicker and there began to come through to Poland, our land of the fields, the news that the country lands of the Ukraine were ablaze. Then it was heard that Kiev had fallen, then Lvov, the city of the Lion, and now there was naught between the savage band of warriors and the fair city of Krakow save a few peaceful villages and fertile fields.

The Tartars came through the world like a horde of wild beasts. They left not one thing alive nor one green blade of wheat standing. They were short, dark men of shaggy beards and long hair twisted into little braids, and they rode on small horses which they covered with trophies that they had gained in war. Brave they were as lions, courageous they were as great dogs, but they had hearts of stone and knew not mercy, nor pity, nor tenderness, nor God. On their horses they carried round shields of leather and iron, and long spears often trailed from their saddles. About their shoulders and thighs they wore skins of animals. Some decorated their ears with golden rings—here and there one wore a gold ring in the nose. When they traveled, the dust rose high into the sky from beneath the hoofs of their little horses, and the thunder of the hoofbeats could be heard many miles away. They were so numerous that it took days for the whole horde to pass any one given point, and for miles behind the army itself rumbled carts bearing slaves, provisions, and booty—usually gold.

Before them went always a long, desperate procession of country people driven from their humble homes by the news of the coming terror; they had already said farewell to the cottages where they lived, the parting from which was almost as bitter as death. So it has always been in time of war that the innocent suffer most—these poor, helpless peasants with their carts and horses and geese and sheep trudging along through the dust to escape, if God so willed, the terrible fate which would befall them were they left behind. There were old people in that procession too feeble to be stirring even about a house, mothers nursing children, women weak with sickness, and men brokenhearted at the loss of all that a lifetime of labor had brought.

Children dragged themselves wearily along beside them, often bearing their pets in their arms.

To this company Krakow opened her gates, and prepared for defense. Many of the nobility and rich citizens had, in the meantime, fled to the west or taken refuge in monasteries far to the north. The brothers of the monastery at Zvierzyniec, a short distance outside the city, took in all the refugees that the building could accommodate, and then prepared to stand siege. But the great, weary, terror-mad mob that had fled ahead of the band of Tartars was content enough to make the city itself its destination. And once within its walls all turned their faces toward the south. For there, in the south of the city, towering on its rocky hill high over the Vistula River, was the great, irregular, turreted mass that was the Wawel—the fortress and castle of the kings of Poland from the time of Krakus, the legend king, and the home of the dukes and nobles who formed the king's court.

It had been decided to make no attempt to defend the city outside the castle gates, since that would entail a great loss of life; and so for several days the city dwellers who remained and these refugees from all the country about poured into the fortification and were housed inside its walls. The old castle gates which were then on Castle Highway opposite the Church of St. Andrew were at last shut and barricaded, and the walls were manned with citizen soldiery prepared to give their lives for the protection of the city and their families.

The Tartars fell upon the city in the night and, after burning the outlying villages, pillaged the districts that lay about the churches of St. Florian, St. John, and the Holy Cross. The whole night long was one of hideous sounds—the crackling and fury of flames, the snarling and yelling of the enemy when they found that the prey had fled, their roars of triumph when they came upon gold and treasure. As morning dawned the watchers from the Wawel looked out over the town and saw but three churches not already in flames. These were the Church of Our Lady Mary near the great market, the Church of St. Andrew, with its stalwart towers, at the Castle Gate, and the Church of St. Adalbert in the market place. Already a colony of Jews in the Black Village had perished, also those refugees and town dwellers who had not rushed inside the walls of defense. There remained but one man—or rather, a youth—still alive in the midst of all that destruction.

He was the trumpeter of the Church of Our Lady Mary, and he had taken solemn oath to sound the trumpet each hour of the day and night from a little balcony high up on the front of the church. As the first golden rays of the sun changed the Vistula from a dark line to a plash of dancing gold, he mounted this balcony to sound the Heynal —the hymn to Our Lady which every trumpeter in the church had in the past sworn to play each hour of the day and night—"until death." He felt with a strange joy the glow of the sun as it fell upon him that morning, for the night had been very dark both with its own shadow and with the gloomy blackness of men's ruthlessness.

About his feet, down in the town highway, stood groups of short, fierce men gazing up at him curiously. Here and there the roof of a house was shooting upward in flames and belching forth clouds of black smoke. Hundreds of dwellings lay charred and ruined by the conflagration. He was alone in the midst of a terrible enemy—he might have fled on the previous day and gained the castle with the refugees and the town dwellers, but he had been true to his oath and remained at his post until he should be driven away. Now it was too late to retreat.

He was a very young man, perhaps nineteen or twenty, and wore a dark cloth suit that was caught at the knees with buckles, like the knickerbockers of a later generation; dark, thick hose extended from the knees to the tops of his soft, pointed sandals, and a short coat falling just below the waist was held together in front by a belt. The head covering was of leather and something like a cowl; it fell clear to his shoulders and ran up over the head in such a way that only his face and a bit of hair were visible.

My mother and sister are safe, he thought. May God be praised for that! They are gone these ten days and must be now with the cousins in Moravia.

It came to him then what a sweet thing life is. The sun over the Vistula was now reflected in the windows of the Cathedral of the Wawel, where the priests were already saying mass. At the tops of all the gates he could see guards in full armor, upon which the sunlight flashed. A banner with a white eagle hung in the air above the gate at the great draw.

Poland lives, he thought.

And then it came to him, young as he was, that he was part of the glorious company of Polish men that was fighting for all Christendom against brutal and savage invaders. He had not seen much of death before that minute—he had heard of it only as something vague. And now, he himself was perhaps going out to meet it, because of his oath, because of his love for the Church, because of his love for Poland.

I shall keep my word, he mused. If I die it shall be for that. My word is as good as my life.

Had a painter caught his expression then, he would have caught only the expression of a very great peace—an expression that signified somehow that God was very close. There was no moment of weakness, no faltering, no suffering even—for he did not think of what might come after his duty was performed. The sand in the hourglass already marked the hour for the trumpet to sound.

"Now, for Poland and Our Lady, I will sound the Heynal," he said, and raised the trumpet to his lips.

Softly he blew at first—then, thrilled with a sense of triumph, he felt in his heart a joy that was almost ecstatic. He seemed to see in a vision that though he might now die alone and for naught save what perhaps some scoffing ones might call a foolish honor, still that bravery was to descend as a heritage to the people to whom he belonged, and was to become a part of their spirit, their courage, their power of everlasting—all this that moment brought.

A Tartar below crouched to his bow and drew back the arrow as far as he could draw. The string whirred. The dark shaft flew like a swift bird straight for the mark. It pierced the breast of the young trumpeter when he was near the end of his song—it quivered there a moment and the song ceased. But, still holding to the trumpet, the youth fell back against the supporting wall and blew one last glorious note; it began strongly, trembled, and then ceased—broken like the young life that gave it birth—and at that moment those below applied the torch to the wooden church, and it, too, rose in flames to Heaven, with the soul of the youth among them.

1

The Man Who Wouldn't Sell His Pumpkin

It was in late July of the year 1461 that the sun rose one morning red and fiery as if ushering in midsummer's hottest day. His rays fell upon the old city of Krakow and the roads leading up to it, along which rolled and rocked a very caravan of peasants' wagons. They were drawn mostly by single horses hitched into place by the side of a rough pole that served for shaft; for wheels there were stout pieces of board nailed tightly together and cut round about, baked with fire at the rim to harden them; for body they had but rude cross boards as a floor, with sides and ends of plaited willow reeds, so that the wagons had the appearance of large baskets traveling on wheels. As they moved along a road often rough from holes and stones, out through fields sometimes, and even across streams, the wagons pitched about like little boats on a windswept sea.

In many cases the drivers were walking alongside the carts, flicking their long whips now and then above the horses' backs to give the animals a little encouragement, while upon the seats sat the patient figures of women and children.

In the wagon was all manner of merchandise—vegetables, flowers, ducks, hens and geese, pigs, butter and milk. Here a driver was conveying a load of skins, here one had nothing but black earth for enriching city gardens. Another, driving a load of poultry, wore around his neck, like beads, garland after garland of dried mushrooms strung upon strings. At the back of the picture rose the foothills of the Carpathians, misty and golden in the early sun, and at a distance the Vistula River curved like a silver bracelet about the Wawel Hill. All about was the early-morning smell of wet grass and fresh earth and growing things.

Market day had begun. All night some of these wagons had been traveling along the highways that spread out from the great highway that was the Krakow, Tarnov, Lvov, Kiev route. Some had been on the march for two days and two nights, so distant were the borders of the province. Here were men and women in town dress from the larger centers, here were barefooted peasants in long coats and round hats, here were peasant women in rough garments but with head scarfs and shawls of dazzling colors, here were the inhabitants of a Jewish village, twelve men in black robes and black hats, with the characteristic orthodox curls hanging down in front of their ears.

Here were boys belonging to the retinue of a local *szlachcic*, or country gentleman, their leather costumes showing up to advantage beside the rather dingy dress of the male portion of the peasantry. Here and there were women with little babies, here and there were old people trudging by the sides of their wagons up to market, as they had done for thirty or forty years past.

But every man in that caravan carried some sort of weapon, either a short knife at the belt, or quarterstaff in the hand, or huge-headed ax at the bottom of the wagon. For thieves were abroad in great number at times of market, and it was even said that there were country gentlemen of ruined fortune who were not above recouping themselves now and then at the expense of some such caravan. Usually, however, it was on the return trip that the thieves were numerous, for then each villager and peasant had gold or silver as the result of the day's bargaining.

Although practically all these wagons carried cargoes of goods, there was one which seemed strangely empty for market day. It had two horses instead of the usual one, its shaft pole was stouter than those of the other wagons, its occupants were better dressed than the peasants and seemed somehow not like actual workers of the soil. In it rode the driver, a man of perhaps forty-five years, a woman—his wife—some ten years younger, and a boy, who sat at the open end of the wagon, dangling his legs above the dirt and mud of the highway.

"Now, wife," said the man, snapping a long whip at the off horse—his wife was sitting beside him on a rude seat at the front of the wagon— "that high tower you see is a watch tower on the Wawel Hill of Krakow. Should we go as flies the stork, we should reach there by the eighth hour. See, in the distance are the two towers of the Church of Our Lady. It is a welcome sight to my eyes after these three weeks on a rocking cart."

The woman threw back a gray hood from her face and looked ahead with longing eyes. "It is Krakow, then," she said, "the city of my mother. Often has she told me of its glory, and yet I never had hoped to see it. God knows I wish I might see it differently and with less pain in my heart. But God gives, and man receives, and we are here at last."

"Yes," said the man.

For a long time they traveled along in silence. The man was musing on his early experiences in Krakow, the woman on her lost home in the Ukraine, and the boy letting his imagination run riot in speculation as to the sights that he should see in the great city.

Their thoughts were brought suddenly from their own affairs to a commotion among the carts behind them. Drivers were reining in their horses and swinging them to the left of the road, narrow as it was, in order to let someone pass. The man whose thoughts had been thus interrupted turned around, trying to discern who it might be who was pushing forward through the long line of carts, and in a moment he saw that it was a rider on a small horse.

"Way, way," the rider was shouting. "Do you peasants think that the whole road belongs to you? . . . Stay on your farm, where you belong," he shouted angrily at a peasant driver whose horse reared suddenly from the edge of the road to the middle. "Give me room to pass. You have no business on the highroad with an animal that jumps about like that."

"I had gone in the ditch else," replied the peasant without surliness.

The rider glanced sharply at the contents of the man's wagon, and being assured that it contained nothing but fresh straw to be sold to brickmakers, dashed ahead until he was even with the cart which held the man and woman and boy.

The last named had been watching his advance curiously. Now this boy, Joseph Charnetski, was in his fifteenth year. He was not by any means handsome, though he could not be called ugly. His hair and his eyes were dark, and his face was somewhat round and very pleasant. He wore rather rich, though travel-soiled, nether garments, not leather like those of the retainers, nor of coarse sacking like the peasants' clothes, but of a good quality of homespun, and a thick, buttoned coat of the same material, which fell skirtlike nearly to the knees. On his feet were brown leather boots, whose tops were soft and loose, and so high that they reached almost to the bottom of the coat. On his head he wore a round hat like a turban.

The instant the rider perceived the boy, "*Chlopak, chlopak* [Boy, boy]," he exclaimed in a rather croaky voice, "tell your old man to hold his horses. You come and hold mine."

The boy obeyed, but as he leaped from the wagon and grasped at the horse's bit thong, he came to the conclusion that the stranger was no friend. In those days when the world was just emerging from a period of darkness and cruelty, it was a necessity that each man should be constantly upon his guard against other men. Robbers abounded—jealous friends often descended to mean tricks; men of noble birth and breeding thought nothing of defrauding poor peasants, and among the poor peasants themselves were those who would commit crimes for the sake of gold.

Therefore when Joseph grasped at the horse's bit rein he had already come to the conclusion, perhaps from something in the stranger's looks or speech or manner, that he was one to be treated with caution. He was attired in a retainer's suit of thick cloth. The jacket was short but concealed a coat of very light chain armor beneath. He wore for breeches not knickerbockers but a single leather garment that combined doublet and hose in one. The cap was round, with a hanging jewel, probably glass, dangling behind against his neck.

It was the face, however, that betrayed the soul beneath. It was a dark, oval, wicked face—the eyes were greenish and narrow and the eyebrow line above them ran straight across the bridge of the nose, giving the effect of a monkey rather than a man. One cheek was marked with a buttonlike scar, the scar of the button plague that is so common in the lands east of the Volga, or even the Dnieper, and marks the bearer as a Tartar or a Cossack or a Mongol. The ears were low set and ugly. The mouth looked like the slit that boys make in the pumpkins they carry on the eve of Allhallows. Above the mouth was a cropped mustache which hung down at the ends and straggled into a scanty beard. The man carried at his waist a short curved sword and from the inside of his jacket could be seen protruding the jeweled handle of an Oriental dagger.

No sooner had the boy caught at his rein than the man was off his horse and with a leap had gained the wagon. Joseph's father reached quickly under the wagon seat for a short cross-hilted sword.

"Not one step nearer," he shouted as the man came toward him with hand outstretched as if to take his hand. "Who you may be I know not, but I stand as a Christian till I find out what your errand is."

The stranger stopped, smiled at the ready sword still in its scabbard, though with a sudden respect in his smile, then pulled off his hat and made a bow. "I take it that you are Andrew Charnetski," he said.

"You take too much," answered the driver. "To strangers I am Pan[1] Andrew Charnetski."

The stranger bowed again. "I spoke as to an equal," he said. "I am Stefan Ostrovski of Chelm. But now I am come from Kiev, where I have been on state business. It is known that one Muscovite has some important business with our Lithuanian provinces, and I, though I may not say by whom, was sent to learn—" He broke off suddenly, as if wishing to give the impression that his business was such that he might not speak of it in public fashion. "But on my way home, men told me that

[1] Pan is a formal Polish term signifying Sir or Mr.

a band of Tartars had come north from the Krim, pillaging much of the country about. Among the houses which they had burned and the fields which they had destroyed were the house and fields of one Andrew Charnetski—nay, I ask pardon—of Pan Andrew Charnetski, who was reported to have escaped with his wife and son in the direction of Krakow, where they were said to have friends. This being true, and since I was traveling in the same direction, I sought a description of Pan Andrew and his family, and this morning when I saw a true Ukrainian cart, drawn by two horses and not by one, and bearing a man and woman and boy such as had been described to me, I took the assurance to present myself and make my greetings to you."

Pan Charnetski scrutinized the face, the clothing, and the figure of the stranger closely. "The half is not yet told," he said.

"Nay," answered the other, "but the rest is perhaps a tale for you and me behind some heavy door when we reach the city of Krakow just ahead. I have heard—" He spoke significantly; then with his hands he described a circle in the air.

Charnetski watched him with his eyelids drawn half shut so that he could focus his attention upon the man and see naught of the world outside. His heart was not so cold and steady, however, as one might think from looking at his calm, composed features. In truth, at the stranger's gesture his heart was beating a tattoo against his ribs. He knew that almost every word the man had uttered was false; he knew that his name was not Ostrovski, even though there had been members of that family in Chelm—not one feature of the man's countenance was Polish. And there was that in the tone of the last words that had suggested a threat. Charnetski realized also that here was no chance meeting. It was fourteen days and more since they had left the border. This man, he reasoned, had followed them all that distance, or had perhaps been sent by some person of higher rank to intercept them before they gained entrance to the city.

"You have heard naught that concerns me," he answered shortly. "And now, since the carts are leaving me behind, will you kindly return to your horse? I have nothing to say that will be of importance to you, nor do you interest me in any way."

Charnetski spoke truly, for the carts ahead were already some distance away and the drivers behind were shouting at him angrily for blocking the traffic.

"On the contrary," answered the stranger, "you have that which interests me greatly. And I will not leave you until we are safe behind some door in the city. Here, boy," he shouted at Joseph, "lead my horse along behind the wagon, for I intend to ride the rest of the way."

Pan Charnetski's cheeks blazed. "Now, by the lightning, you make yourself too free here," he articulated. "State what business you have quickly and be done."

The man glanced around the cart and he saw on the wooden floor just in front of the driver's seat a huge yellow pumpkin. "Ha," he said, "a pumpkin, and at this time of the year. I suppose they raise pumpkins in the winter on the steppe. What shall be the price of that pumpkin?"

"It is not for sale," answered Charnetski.

"No?"

"I said no."

"What if I offer its weight in gold?"

"All's one."

"You will not sell?"

"I tell you, *no.*"

"Then"—the stranger drew his sword quickly—"then you will fight for it!" And he stepped forward toward the driver.

Charnetski hesitated no longer. In the flash of an eye he had vaulted across the seat, dodged a blow of the saber, and caught the stranger's right wrist in a grip of steel. The sword dropped with a clang. Charnetski did not let the man go, however. He threw his left hand into the small of the stranger's leg and with clutch upon arm and leg hoisted him high and tossed him out of the cart. He fell in the mud, sputtering with rage and calling curses of every description upon Charnetski's head. And at this minute Joseph, with admirable foresight, swung the man's horse about and struck him smartly upon the right flank. The horse reared and capered, then dashed off down the road in the direction from which the wagons had come; at the same instant the boy leaped upon the cart and shouted to his father, who climbed back to the seat and swung the long lash over the horses' heads. They were off in a second, leaving the stranger in the middle of the highway, turning now to the right and now to the left as if uncertain whether to pursue his horse or his enemy. And Charnetski, swinging about, picked up the sword from the bottom of the cart and hurled it into the road.

Some time later they reached the Kazimierz, the Jewish city founded by King Kazimir more than one hundred years earlier. Passing through this, they came to the bridge across the Vistula which would admit them to the city of Krakow itself. Finding, however, that this bridge was undergoing repairs, they were forced to take the next bridge to the north; thence they proceeded to the fortified gate called Mikolayska, where they were challenged by the gatekeeper.

2

Krakow

"Charnetski, Christian, wife and son," said Pan Andrew to a custodian who wore light armor and carried a halberd.

He gave them a quick glance and motioned for them to pass. Another man in black peered into the cart to see what was inside, and finding nothing, concluded that these were farm folk come up to the city to buy, and accordingly demanded but a few pieces of iron coin as tax. This paid, they took the road which ran from Mikolayska Gate to the Sukiennice, the old Cloth Hall, which stood then, as it does today, in the very center of the city.

Krakow was flooded with a golden sunlight. Joseph, who saw for the first time a large city, gaped in very astonishment as he glanced left and right about him.

Front and rear, their cart formed part of the long straight train of carts coming to the city loaded with products of the farms. Through this line were breaking from time to time splendid horsemen wearing breastplates of steel that shone like precious metal and carrying long swords dangling from the saddles. One of these men who pushed through the crowd just in front of their horses was so splendidly arrayed that the boy took him for a very high noble, or perhaps the king himself, the peace-loving king, Kazimir Jagiello, the fourth of the name of Kazimir, and he exclaimed:

"That must be the king, Father. See the shining armor and the jewels upon his saddle. And the sword must be of gold, for it shines like fire. And look"—he pointed eagerly—"see the Polish eagle worked in silver upon the saddlecloth. There beyond it is the white knight of Lithuania. Is he not indeed the king?"

"No, son, no. That is but one of the guard that waits on the nobles at the royal castle."

All about them rose in the bright sunlight palaces, churches, towers, battlement walls, and Gothic buildings, as yet for the most part unadorned by the rich sculpture that was to come in a few years under the influence of the Italian Renaissance. In the distance rose against the turquoise-blue sky the cathedral on the Wawel Hill, its Romanesque tower showing high above the city. Close at hand were the two towers of the Church of Our Lady Mary, not as they appear today since the hand of the master architect and of the renowned sculptor Wit Stwosz altered them, but rising unbelfried and uncrowned above the cemetery, where white gravestones clustered at the base of the church.

In the very middle of the market, surrounded by smaller wooden buildings, was the great Cloth

Hall, used for the sale and exchange of cloth goods, already swarming with merchants who had been traveling all night, and for many nights perhaps, in order to close bargains early on market day before the money of purchasers had been spent elsewhere.

Camped in the square outside the Cloth Hall were a number of Tartars who had come from the distant East to sell fine swords and cloths and jewels plundered from Muscovites, or Bulgarians, or Greeks, or other travelers in the steppes. Facing the east as the rising sun had crept over Wawel Hill, they had chanted their morning prayer of praise to the great Allah. Their singing could have been heard mingling with the clashing of the great bell on the Church of Our Lady Mary and the chanted service of the Armenian merchants who had come in from Trebizond and the lands beyond the Black Sea with carpets and spices and fine rugs.

Here for the moment in this great international capital of East and West was worshiped every god that man knows; it might even be said that God himself was worshiped under many names and in many languages and dialects. Here were Turks, Cossacks, Ruthenians, Germans, Flemings, Czechs, and Slovaks, with their wares to sell, and Hungarians with their wines from the mellow plains of Transylvania.

As for money, there might be found zloty and guilder and groschen, silver in bars, and precious stones, also plenty of token "in kind"—that is to say, certain varieties of merchandise such as amber, dates bound in packages, or even vegetables in containers, each of which had a recognized value over all the trade routes of the Hanseatic League. For the League merchants were represented here as well—prosperous Germans or Dutchmen in long robes with fur collars—and they did business in every language known to man.

While the boy drank in these unusual sights on all sides, there suddenly floated down from above the sweet notes of a trumpet. Looking directly upward he could see the golden bell of a trumpet protruding from one of the tower windows of the Church of Our Lady Mary, and as he looked the full dignity of the church burst upon him, its quiet strength which appealed to the eye being strangely mingled in his senses with the trumpet song which fell upon his ears.

There were two towers rising high above the traffic of the street; rising unequally, he now noticed, for the nearer tower seemed a bit squat beside the farther one. It was from the higher tower that the trumpeter was playing.

The tune was a little morning hymn, the Heynal, brought into Poland, some said, in the earliest days of Christianity by missionaries who came from the south. It was a simple little air, intensely sweet and appealing, but at a certain place the trumpeter broke the tune off abruptly, leaving but the echo of an unfinished strain to float down from above. It was as if someone at that moment had taken the trumpet from his lips.

Joseph turned to his father in astonishment. "Isn't he going to finish the song?"

The father smiled. "It is a long story, my son, and one that I will tell you at a later time."

The trumpet sounded again, from another window, then from the farther side, and finally at the north side, toward the Florian Gate. Four times the trumpeter had sounded the Heynal, ending always with the broken note.

"He plays rather poorly," added Pan Charnetski.

Now, though Pan Charnetski was a country gentleman, he was accomplished in many crafts. After having graduated from the University of Krakow, he decided not to remain in one of the professions but rather to live on his father's estate and manage it, as had been the custom for the men in his family. He had retained a love of music, which he had studied in the university, and played well upon brass instruments, the straight trumpet, the curved trumpet, and the trumpet with keys. Therefore when he said that the trumpeter in the tower had not played well he knew of what he was talking.

The cart was now passing close to the Cloth Hall, and Joseph ceased to question his father any further concerning the song with the broken note because of the strange scenes which claimed his attention.

Here stood a group of merchants in bright gowns. Wealthy they must have been because their long coats were of fine cloth, some lined with fur and trimmed with many silks. Beneath the coats were costumes of tight-fitting cloth. Joseph saw one man with the color of the cloth in the trouser of the right leg different from the color of the cloth of the left trouser, which to the boy had a ludicrous look. But when he noticed that many other men wore the same kind of garment, tight-fitting to leg and thigh, and of different color upon each leg, he ceased to smile and began to wonder. The wonder did not leave off for a while, either, for other curiosities in dress caught his eye. The hats and head coverings were in their way as remarkable as the tight garments. Turbans were worn uniformly, some with pointed peaks, others simply masses of gayly colored cloth heaped up high on the head in twists and folds; grotesque ornaments, too, were worn on the head—one man even had a stuffed or an imitation rooster, with legs and comb and all, perched on the crown of his high hat. The merchants wore curious leather footgear, most of the sandals being of soft leather with long, twisted points. One man had sticks thrust into the leather at the toes, making his sandals appear at least two feet long.

At the stalls around the Cloth Hall were all manner of wares, which the sellers were advertising with loud cries. Here was a grain counter with different colored grains in open sacks. A woman in a blue gown which hung from a yoke at the shoulder, and with a piece of cloth of the same color wound deftly around her head for a hat, was selling a few grains of corn to a traveling musician. He wore a long yellow garment all of a piece, including head covering like a cowl, and falling to the knees, below which the legs and feet were bare. This garment was caught at the waist by a bright yellow belt. He carried under one arm a bagpipe with three protruding tubes, two for music, if it might be called such, and one for his mouth. In one hand he held a pouch of leather into which the woman was slipping grains of corn.

The Charnetskis drove by the stalls and shops of the glove makers, where there were women working and buying, all dressed in bright-colored gowns; past the needle makers in leather aprons, who sprawled over benches; past the sword makers, with their neat forges and rows of shining steel blades; past the tub makers, who were assembling wooden staves into tub bodies; past the smiths in their long black aprons, leading horses into position where they could be shod. Here and there the red signs of the barber and bloodletter, here and there the huge flasks of green and blue denoting the stores of the apothecaries. True Catholics had upon the walls of their shops an ikon or a picture of the Holy Mother of God from the sacred shrine of Chenstohova; almost every merchant had some distinctive figure above the door of his shop to distinguish it from his neighbor's; for example there was a hatter with the sign "Under the White Elephant," and there was a shoemaker who had a stone head of Kazimir the Great for the satisfaction of himself and his customers. The numbering of public buildings was not known in that age, and buildings were distinguished by some such emblem, which usually stood above the outer gate or door.

Everywhere could be heard the cries of vendors

shouting or singing their wares or professions, the flower girls, the knife sharpener, the baker's boy, and the butcher's apprentice.

"*Co brakuje, co brakuje?*" they all shouted in a chorus. "What do you lack? What do you lack?"

Occasionally, to Joseph's delight, a monkey could be seen, brought here by traders from the east or south, one playing around a booth, another carried, much bedecked with ribbons, in the arms of some merchant's or perhaps burgomaster's lady.

Once or twice amid the clamor of the market rang the clanking of chains as poor wretches about to be fastened to the church walls by iron collars, or stuck in the pillory, or perhaps even to suffer a worse fate, were marched to the church for a last prayer before the sentence of the law was passed upon them. Life was a precarious thing in many ways in those days, and men and women for very slight offenses were beheaded or banished or thrown into prisons.

Now they passed a procession of pilgrims on the way to some shrine, men and women from the villages dressed in their good clothes with the parish priest marching ahead of them and leading the chant which they were singing. The cross bearer was a young man with stalwart shoulders and bright eyes; he had need of his strength, too, for he had sworn to carry the holy image of Our Lord from his native village to Chenstohova, which was many miles distant. This company had already been on the road about ten days. There were boys and girls, too, in the procession, and some had their minds upon serious things, but others were looking for the first time upon the glory of medieval Krakow, and would no doubt in their prayers ask forgiveness for too much attention to worldly things.

The cart turned into Grodzka, or Castle, Street, after leaving the market place and went directly toward the Wawel. Near the Wawel Pan Andrew swung the horses to the right and passed through a city gate and into a meadowy lane. In front of a large rambling palace that stood there, he drew up by the side of the road and leaped to the ground not far from a pair of iron gates that marked the entrance. At these gates he was accosted by an armed guard who, with a rather hostile air, blocked the entrance completely with his spear.

"What do you want?" he asked sharply.

"I seek Pan Andrew Tenczynski."

The guard shouted something, whereat five men in armor came running from a little house near the gate.

"Surround him," said the guard. This was done, much to the astonishment of Pan Andrew. "One of you run to the house and call the captain," next ordered the guard. "Tell him that a countryman is here demanding to see Pan Andrew Tenczynski."

Pan Charnetski, trying to force his way out of the circle, was pushed back into the center by one of the armed men. At that he raised his voice in anger:

"Who are you that dare detain me here? I am Pan Andrew Charnetski, first cousin to the Tenczynskis and proprietor of an estate in the Ukraine. I demand that you confront me with an officer in authority and not treat me like one come here as an enemy."

The men of the guard looked at each other in astonishment. Was it possible that this man did not know the truth—the report of which had already spread over the greater portion of Poland?

The captain came in a moment with the returning soldier. He broke through the ring and walked straight up to Pan Charnetski.

"What is your business here?" There was a certain pleasantness and courtesy in his voice that made Pan Andrew forget his anger for the moment.

"You have a civil tongue, young man," he answered. "I take it that you are in command here?"

"I am."

"Then I will tell you, as I have told your soldiers, that I am Pan Andrew Charnetski, come this day from the Ukraine to see my cousin Pan Andrew Tenczynski on important business."

"You come too late," answered the captain. "It is strange that you have not heard, for this news is now all about the country. Pan Andrew Tenczynski lives no longer. His kin have departed from the city for a time, and may return I know not when. I am here for the observance of order, for the protection of the estate against enemies of the family."

Pan Andrew started. "My cousin is dead—and how?"

"It was like to nothing the city has seen these many years. For a long time there had been hot blood between the tradesmen and nobles. The issue came to a head through the dissatisfaction of

Pan Tenczynski over some piece of armor that he had bidden a smith to make. He not only took the tradesman to task but refused to pay for the work he had done, whereat the whole guild rose against him. They pursued him through the streets and killed him in the Church of the Franciscans, where he had sought shelter. It was a sad and grievous thing, and his family for fear of the mob fled the city. The gentle Elizabeth, our queen—and may the blessing of Heaven be upon her!—hates all strife that may result in the shedding of blood, and she it was who persuaded our king to make peace between the townsfolk and nobles. He sent us here to protect this house, to be a guarantee against the shedding of any blood, for there are many who would willingly pillage this dwelling and kill the servants that are still here. We are but acting upon orders when we detain all persons who seek entrance here, and for the execution of these orders you must give us your pardon, since we seek but to avert further bloodshed."

It seemed to Pan Andrew at that moment as if heaven had fallen about his ears.

"Let me give to Pan one piece of advice," continued the captain.

"Most willingly will I receive it," said Pan Andrew thoughtfully.

"Get yourself from the city as quickly as possible if you be of any blood ties with the Tenczynskis, or else, if you stay, change your name and manner of speech lest some assassin make a mark of you for the benefit of his party. . . . I greet you then with a hail, as is befitting between equal Pans,

and request that, for your own safety, you depart
quickly."

"But—I must remain here. A band of pillagers,
I know not whom exactly, though I think them the
paid robbers of someone in high authority, have
burned my house in the Ukraine and left not one
stone upon another. My fields are ruined as well,
and I am here to take refuge with my kinsmen, to
bring them word of something very secret, which
must go at once to the ears of the king himself."

"Alas," answered the captain, "I can give you
but little help. The king is at this moment in
Torun, where there are said to be plans against the
military order of the Knights of the Cross—for he
seeks there in the north peace at all odds. When he
will return I know not, perhaps in a month, perhaps in a year. If you would await him here, I
would, if I were you, settle in this town and take
another name. Later there will come a retribution
for these dark deeds against the Tenczynski family,
and there will be more crows about the gallows."

Saying which, he turned away and called the
guard again to its post.

Pan Andrew, however, stood motionless for a
few seconds. The thoughts fairly burned in his
brain. His friends, protectors, gone! The king
away, he himself a fugitive here no less than in the
Ukraine. From every side enemies pressed upon
him, and what had he done to deserve such a fate?
He was in a predicament even without this compli-
cation, for here he was in a great city where he had
not a single friend. He had but little money, for
what he had gathered had been invested year by

year in his house and lands in the Ukraine. There were his wife and his son to be put in a place of shelter, and not only were the means lacking but there was even peril at every hand. Behind him at the gates of the city had appeared one foe—here in the city there were apparently many others. What to do? . . . Well. . . . Let God give. . . . There would be something.

Aimlessly he got into the wagon, turned it about, and made for the market again. There at least they might spend the day, procure water for the horses, and buy a little of something to eat. He found a place near one of the springs, unloosed the horses with the help of his son, and let them crop the short grass that grew near one edge of the market place, watering them with buckets that he filled at the spring.

Not until then did he seek comfort and counsel from his wife, who had always been his solace at such times; throwing himself down beside her on the wagon seat, he told her the story of his late discoveries, the absence of the king, the death of his kinsman. For a second the woman's heart quailed before the fresh difficulties, but she forgot self at the look in her husband's face. Her quiet reply, "We will wait, for God is in the waiting," filled him with courage again.

Joseph, however, was at that age when no sky remains long clouded. His heart had been beating fast with excitement ever since the sight of the city's towers had loomed before them in the early morning, and his legs had been itching to get out of the wagon and explore the place. He began by taking a short excursion over to a little building near by, which at first glance had seemed to be a market building, but, when he approached it, proved to be a church with a low dome and round side windows. Although the church was of much interest to those who favored historical lore as being one of the oldest churches in Poland, it did not interest the boy greatly. He scrutinized the beggars at the door, a young boy with but one leg, a woman with a back bent to a curve, an old man with sightless eyes, praying continually, and many other wretched alms seekers. Crossing himself and muttering a prayer for God's helpless creatures, Joseph turned and marched down Grodzka Street in the direction of the Wawel.

He had just come to a cross lane which led on the left to the Church of the Dominicans, and on the right to the Church of All Saints, when he noticed a Tartar boy in the street leading and constantly beating a large Ukrainian wolf dog. The wolf dog was on a leash—he had a strong hand-wrought collar about the neck—and he was turning now and then to glance back at his tormentor, who was plying a short Cossack whip. Joseph watched the boy in amazement, wondering why he had the dog and why he was beating him—as a matter of fact, the boy was acting out of pure viciousness—but neither of these questions found satisfactory solution in Joseph's mind. In a very few minutes, however, another question rose with the suddenness of lightning, a question which required action for a solution, and this action Joseph was able to supply.

For at the moment that the boy and dog were crossing the church lane, there emerged from the farther footwalk a man dressed all in black like a priest, but wearing a collar which was not clerical, since it opened in the front. He did not, however, for the moment attract Joseph's attention; it was his companion that caught and held the boy's gaze. For the companion was a girl of perhaps the same age as Joseph—she was walking by the side of the man in black and now and then grasping at his hand.

Joseph saw the dog no longer. His eyes were riveted on the girl. She seemed to him like an angel taken out of a Christmas play, or a spirit from a Festival of the Three Kings—in truth, she might have been one of those beautiful figures come to life out of the wondrous stained-glass windows in the church. Her hair was light—Joseph's was dark. Her skin was as white as the finest linen, her eyes as blue as the skies above the Vistula; she wore a cloaklike garment of red that fell from her shoulders to her ankles and was girdled at the waist. It was embroidered in blue, with lace at neck and wrists; in front it did not meet completely but showed the second garment that she wore beneath, a mantle of blue that fell in folds even below the outer coat. And as she looked up, the country boy thought that he had never seen anything prettier on earth—so daintily she tripped along that she seemed to walk on clouds. Then for a moment he looked down at his hands, dirty, hard, and grimy; he looked at his clothes and found them dusty and worn after the long journey.

But if he had been in heaven at the sight of the girl, he came back to earth quickly. For the Tartar boy with the dog and the man in black with the girl were close together at the crossing of the roads when suddenly the maddened dog turned desperately at bay upon his tormentor and crouched for a powerful spring. Joseph shouted and rushed forward just as the dog leaped. The Tartar boy dropped the leather thong in a flash and darted down the walk out of reach of the dog's jaws, but leaving directly in his path the man in black and the girl. Blind with fury the dog sprang again, and in an instant he would have come down upon the girl, who happened to be on the outside, had not Joseph at the same moment leaped and caught at the dog's heavy collar.

He had dealt with dogs many times in the Ukraine, and he knew that no dog is vicious if healthy and well treated; therefore there had been no fear in this effort that he made, save for the peril, perhaps, that the dog might mistake him for the boy who had been beating him, and sink his teeth into his flesh.

His fingers caught the collar squarely. The grip held, and he went hurtling through the air like the tail of a skyrocket, as the dog's leap, weighted by this unexpected load, fell short and the girl drew back with a cry. But Joseph and the infuriated animal went rolling to and fro in a wild embrace on the hard surface of the road, he striving to make the beast pay attention to his words, the dog only becoming more and more frightened. But the boy knew, after the first second when all depended upon whether his grip held or not, that everything was safe and he could successfully avoid the paws and teeth of the dog. Thus at a favorable moment he released his hold quickly upon the animal's collar and scrambled to his feet while a very dusty and possibly ashamed wolf dog tore off like a streak of lightning in the direction of the Franciscans' church.

3

The Alchemist

Something heavy but kindly fell upon Joseph's shoulders and something light touched his cheek.

Looking up quickly from a survey of his garments, now more ragged and dusty than ever, he perceived that the weight was the hand of the man in black and that the lightness had been a kiss upon his cheek from the man's companion—her cheeks were flushed and her eyes bright and her lips were still close to him. He was somewhat dazed from the shock of going to earth so quickly with the dog, but he thrilled with pleasure and happiness from the kindly touch and the kiss.

He stepped back to brush himself, and then gazed squarely at the man and girl.

His cheeks grew rosy with that first meeting of eyes. For in the man's there was an ocean of gratitude and a suggestion of a tear, and the girl's eyes blazed forth frank admiration.

"You were so quick," she exclaimed. "Would that I could spring like that. It was brave of you—"

His tongue found no words. Boys of fifteen, even if aged by experience, have little to say when praise is bestowed so freely.

Moreover the man gave him no opportunity. "Remarkable," he said, "remarkable. As swift a leap as I ever saw," and then blinking with his eyes as if the light hurt them, added, "or hope to see."

"It was nothing," Joseph stammered. "Often in the Ukraine I have dispersed dogs in a fight." And then thinking that this perhaps sounded like boasting, said further, "As do many boys of my age in that country."

"From the Ukraine?" The man in black looked at him with interest. "How do you happen to be so far from home?"

"Tartars or Cossacks burned our house. We have been traveling this day more than two weeks in a cart only to find ourselves homeless here. Father had kinsfolk in this city, but the head of the house is dead and the others are away."

"Where are your people now?"

"In the market place."

"H'm," the man muttered to himself, "homeless and in the market place. And what will they do?"

The boy shook his head. "I think that my father will find us some shelter," he said finally. "He was thinking—" He hesitated, for he had been taught never to speak of troubles before strangers, though the girl peered straight into his eyes with great kindness and sweetness.

There is something curious here, thought the man. The boy's face has a high degree of intelligence and his speech is the speech of one who has listened to good words. A noble action this—I think in good faith that the whelp might have had his teeth in the child's throat.

Looking down upon the boy he said, "You have rendered us a noteworthy service, you have saved my niece from much painful injury; will you not accompany us to our home that we may hear your whole story and perhaps in our turn—"

The boy's face reddened. "Nay," he said, "I wish no reward. What I did—"

The girl caught him up. "Indeed you do my uncle wrong. He meant but this: we live humbly, will you not come and rest for a moment until you may join your people?"

"I ask pardon," the boy said quickly.

Whereat the man laughed, for their speech and expression had been overserious for children, though it still was an age when children grew to be men and women often over a single night. In some provinces girls of fourteen or fifteen were considered grown women and even given in marriage. Boys at that age had seen much of the rough side of life, of war and battle and cruelty.

"I will go with you," Joseph added, kissing the cuff of the gown of the man in black as he had always been taught to do in his home.

They turned to the left past the Church of the Franciscans, to the right through a short lane, and then to the left again into the most curious street of the world of that day.

It was the Street of the Pigeons, famed throughout all Europe as the dwelling place of scholars, astrologers, magicians, students, and likewise doctors, brothers of the Church, and masters of the seven arts. In the worst end of the street, the upper end near the city wall, clustered the squalid dwelling places that were once the homes of Jewish refugees, fleeing from persecution in all parts of the world. Terrible poverty had existed there, and when the Jewish inhabitants finally moved to their own city, Kazimierz, across the river, the buildings which they left were scarcely fit for human beings to live in. They were, in the first place, very old and out of repair—they were built for the most part of wood, though the fronts on the streets were sometimes of brick covered with rough cement or mortar. The upper stories usually overhung, and the roofs were covered with loose boards nailed in place, serving instead of tiles or shingles. Rickety staircases on the outside of these buildings led from the streets or from interior courts up to the dwelling places on the third and fourth floors, where, at the time of this story, lived family literally heaped upon family in terrible disorder and poverty.

Thieves and murderers crouched there in hiding during the day, bands of lawless men had their haunts there in cellar or attic or other den. A fire in the year 1407 had swept through this street and through St. Ann's, clearing out many of these undesirable places, but unfortunately not destroying all of them.

In the lower end of the street on the side toward the University of Krakow there was more respectability, since students and masters of the university inhabited there. A large students' *bursar*, or dormitory, stood near the corner where Jagiellonska now meets the Street of the Pigeons. In this lived many students; others put up near by in groups or with private families, since it was not until late in the 1490's that the authorities compelled the students to live in university buildings.

The prestige of the various colleges and the reputation of the men who taught there had drawn to Krakow not only genuine students but also many of the craft that live by their wits in all societies, in all ages—fortune tellers and astrologers, magicians and palmists, charlatans, necromancers, and fly-by-nights who were forever eluding the authorities of the law. Here, somewhere on the Street of the Pigeons, they all found lodging.

In the rooms above the street, in the kitchens beneath the street, these men plied their trades. Self-termed astrologers read in the stars the destinies of the gullible; they foretold happiness to trusting peasant girls who came to them for advice in their love matters; they prophesied disaster to merchants who, held by fear, might be induced to part with much money; they cheated, they robbed, and often on provocation they killed, until after many years they gave the street a certain unsavory reputation. Against the machinations of these men the influence of the university was ever working, and the first great blow that many of these magic crafts and black arts received was struck by Nicholas Kopernik, better known as Copernicus, many years later, when Joseph Charnetski was a very old man; Copernicus, working with rough implements, even before the telescope had been invented,

proved to men for the first time that the heavenly
bodies, stars and planets, move in the skies according to well-fixed and definitely determined laws,
subject only to the will of the Creator of the universe, and that they have nothing to do with the
destinies of individuals.

All about them in the street flitted men dressed
in long robes like that of the guardian of the little
girl, though all the robes were not alike. Some were
clerical, with closed front and collar; others were
open and flowing, with great sleeves like a bishop's
gown; some were of blue, some were of red, some
were of green. Joseph noticed one robe of ermine
over which was worn a chain of heavy gold, at the
end of which hung suspended a great amethyst
cross.

They passed a house, part wood and part stone,
where were gathered at opened doors a great group
of young men in plain black robes, much less
sumptuous than some others which they had seen,
all the members of the group engaged in a lively
altercation, as the guardian informed the boy and
girl, concerning the movement of the stars. One
was contending that the firmament of stars moved
for one hundred years to the west—another (and
this was backed by a written argument from the
old Alphonsian tables from Spain) that the stars
moved constantly in one direction without change.

Passing this group they came to a dwelling the
front of which was stone. The door was set back
from the street and flanked by short projecting buttresses on either side, put there as if to caution the
emerging inhabitant to look carefully to right and

left before proceeding—a caution not unwise at night. The windows above were not only crossed by wooden shutters that opened and closed like doors, but also barred with iron. The man in black took from the folds of his gown a huge brass key, which he fitted into the outside door, turned it in the lock with some labor, and then threw the portal open.

They stepped over a small board which served as a threshold, and passed through a dark passageway which led to an open court. At the end of the court was the flat wall of a monastery, without windows or doors. On the right was a low, one-story building, and on the left rose a ramshackle structure of wood, four stories high. Outside this building, leading to the apartments on the second and third floors, was a wooden staircase hitched to the wall by wooden clutch supports and strengthened by a single wooden upright. In the middle of the court was an old well with a bucket on a rope attached to a wheel.

The staircase creaked as they ascended, and seemed to Joseph to swing just a little. It gave him such a dizzy sensation that he clutched at the wall, fearful lest the whole structure should become loose and topple down. But the man only smiled as he saw the boy's sudden movement and assured him that the staircase was safe enough. They went up one flight, past the first landing, and then on to the second. Here they stopped and the man reached into his gown for another key, a smaller one this time.

Just as they were entering the apartment on the

third floor opposite this landing, Joseph noticed that there was still one more floor above them, even though the main staircase ended with the third floor. The entrance to this top floor, which appeared to have been at one time a loft or store-room, was gained by climbing a crude ladderlike staircase with a single rail, which was fastened at a slight angle against the wall. The door to which these steps led was directly above the farther end of the landing, and to Joseph's surprise, appeared to be of metal. From its shape and size the boy decided that it was a window that had been changed into an entrance, while at its right a square aperture had been cut in the wall, probably for the purpose of giving light. In an instant they were in the apartment where the man and girl lived, and Joseph had no further chance to study the loft which in some unexplainable manner had aroused his curiosity.

This apartment was stuffy and poorly lighted, but the furnishings were not poor. There were tapestries and great oaken chairs, a heavy table in the middle of the room, several huge chests, and a sideboard upon which some silver glistened.

The girl ran quickly to a shutter and threw it open, whereupon the light streamed in through a myriad of small glass panes set in lead. Quickly she set before Joseph and the man in black, small goblets which she filled with wine; a few pieces of broken bread were placed before them on the table, and they all ate, Joseph rather voraciously, although striving to disguise his hunger.

"Now tell us your story," the man bade him.

Joseph related it briefly, emphasizing for the most part the arrival of his father and mother and himself in the city that morning, and the dilemma that faced them in procuring lodgings.

The man in the black robe listened attentively, and when the boy had finished he struck the table a light blow. "I think I have it," he said. "Wait here for me and take what refreshment you will. I will be back in a few moments."

He went out through the door and hurried down the stairs to one of the apartments below.

The girl pushed her chair closer to Joseph's and looked up into his eyes.

"What is your name?" she asked.

"I am Joseph Charnetski."

"Joseph," she said. "I like the name much. Mine is Elzbietka."

"My father is Andrew Charnetski," continued Joseph, "and we lived in the country of the black lands in the Ukraine. It was lonely in our neighborhood, for the nearest neighbor was sixty staja away, yet we never felt fear of Cossack or Tartar, though others did, for my father always treated them well. We were therefore surprised not long ago when there came to us a former servant, a friendly Tartar, who said that we were in some danger, and although my father laughed, I know that he gave the report some credence, since he took the Tartar aside and talked with him privately for a long time. He is not one to reveal his fear, however, and we remained in our house as before, with the warning all but forgotten by my mother and me.

"Then one night before we went to bed, my mother, who was working upon some sewing, saw a man's face peeping in through the thatch at one corner of our house. It was a face that she had never seen before; it was not one of the servants of our place or any place next to ours; it was a villainous face and it made such an impression on her that she screamed aloud, alarming us all."

"Yes?" The blue eyes were full of interest.

"That night my father came into the room where I was sleeping, bade me dress quickly, and in a short time led me and my mother through a little door in the rear of the house that I had never seen opened before, since it had always been fastened with nails. Outside this door we found ourselves in a passageway dug out of the earth like a cave, and through this we crept until we emerged into a shed some distance from the other dwellings where two of our best horses were hitched to a cart. That my father had already taken such precautions unknown to us assured me that he had feared something, the nature of which he had kept from us."

"But you know now?"

"Nay—the most curious part is yet to come. My mother and I climbed into the wagon, where a goodly supply of food had been stored, while my father, moving swiftly, wielded a forked stick with such effect, in one corner of the shed, that he soon unearthed a pile of vegetables which had been covered over with tree branches and leaves in order to preserve them. I thought at the time that he was about to put some of them into our wagon for food, but to my surprise he chose only one."

"And that—"

"A pumpkin."

"A *pumpkin!* But why—"

"I know no more about it than you. When everything else in our wagon had been eaten, Father refused to give it up—this was ten days later, of course, when we were on the last stages of our journey; and once, indeed this very morning, a man who had evidently pursued us from the Ukraine offered my father the pumpkin's weight in gold in exchange for it—but my father refused."

"Did you learn whose face your mother saw in the thatch?"

"That I did not, but what came later proved that my father had acted wisely in leaving our house secretly and in a hurry. For when we stopped in a village a few days later to rest our horses, we saw a neighbor who had traveled from our part of the country on horseback. He had passed our place on the day after we left. Every building had been burned to the ground, he told us, and the land itself looked as if a battle had raged there; the wheat was down and the crops were burned, and holes had been dug everywhere, as if the invaders had hunted for hidden treasure."

"Your father has the pumpkin now?"

"It is safe in his possession—though why he refused its weight in gold I cannot see. But I think he would not be pleased that I have told all this about it, although I know that the secret is safe with you. Now tell me something of yourself. This man whom you called uncle—is he your father's brother?"

"That he is. My mother and father died in the plague that spread through the town when I was small. He is a master of arts in the university and a very great scholar," she added proudly. "His name is Nicholas Kreutz, and among those most famed in the university in alchemy he is indeed the greatest. He is not a servant of the Church, though a good Christian, and he seeks, as do many others, the secrets of his craft."

The scholar-alchemist appeared suddenly in the doorway and smiled at them.

"I have just ascertained," he said, seating himself at the table, "that if it pleases your father, there is a haven for you all here in this very house. There is not much to pay, and a shelter, however lowly, is better than the sky when night falls. Your father might sell his pair of horses—horses bring a good price at present, I hear—and he could live here until some suitable employment appears. Unless," he added, "the place is too humble—"

"Indeed that cannot be," said the boy eagerly. "Gladly at this minute will he welcome any roof for the sake of my mother, who is somewhat tired after the long journey from the Ukraine. I cannot go too swiftly to tell him of this news. But only assure me that you are in sober earnest about this matter."

Elzbietka sprang up from her chair. "Did you but know him as well as I, you would not doubt."

At that the alchemist enveloped her with his long arms, from which hung the black sleeves of his gown, until she smiled out from the embrace at

Joseph like one caught between the wings of a great raven or crow.

"Hurry and tell your people," she commanded him, "and bring them back here. Indeed, I never knew what a mother was. If I but please her—"

"That you will," shouted Joseph. "I will go as soon as Pan Kreutz unlocks the door for me below."

"Tell your people that it is the floor beneath us that is unoccupied," directed the alchemist as he let the boy out through the gate. "There are only two rooms there, a large and a small one, but they will serve your purposes for the time, I believe."

Joseph thanked him with all his heart and set out on the run for the market place. The Street of the Pigeons seemed to unwind before him as he ran, and he was soon in the street leading directly to the Cloth Hall.

Turning there, past one corner of the Town Hall, he ran directly by the cloth markets and headed for the little church near which his father had unloosed the horses. But no sooner had his eyes fallen upon the wagon and his father and mother standing in it, than he stopped suddenly in astonishment. Then, like an arrow leaving a bow, he darted forward, for what he saw set his heart beating faster than it had beaten in all that eventful day.

The stranger that they had left in the mud by the roadside that morning stood by the side of the wagon with a crowd of ruffians at his heels, threatening and shouting at Pan Andrew and his wife.

The stranger carried a huge club, and the ruffians, of whom he appeared to be the leader, were armed with staves and stones and were shouting angrily, as if intent on harming the man and woman above them. Pan Andrew, in facing them, had stepped in front of his wife, to shield her if stones were thrown; and the sight of the resistance, and the cries of the leader and his attackers, soon brought a huge crowd surging about the wagon, for it was now close on to noon, and the morning's business of the market was well-nigh finished and many citizens and farmers were eating or resting in the shade of the trees about the square.

Joseph darted through the crowd and leaped up on the wagon, to stand by his father's side.

"Ha, we have the cub as well," shouted the one who had boasted of the name Ostrovski in the early morning. "He is a wizard like unto the father, and a witch like the mother, for it was he who made my horse fly straight up to heaven this morning with a blow upon the flank."

At that, a great skulk in the crowd let fly a stone at the three, which missed Pan Andrew but narrowly.

"Magicians, wizards, witches," hooted the crowd.

"It is the man who is the worst," shouted the self-named Ostrovski. "It is he who hath bewitched my brother and cut off his head and changed the head into a pumpkin. If he be honest, let him deliver that pumpkin over to me in the sight of all, that I may give Christian burial to my brother's brains. . . . An' he will not, let him face my charge. He is a wizard, yea, and one condemned by

Church and court and precept. At him! Kill him!
But save me the pumpkin which is the head of my
brother!"

Absurd as these accusations seem today, they
did not seem so in the fifteenth century. For men
were then but beginning to see the folly of many
superstitions and cruelties that had been prevalent
since the Dark Ages; they believed that certain
persons had malign powers such as could transform others into strange animals; they thought that
by magic, men could work out their spite upon
others in horribly malicious ways; that food could
be poisoned by charms and milk made sour.

And to raise the cry of wizard against a man, no
matter how peace-loving and innocent he might be,
was enough to start rough and brutal men, yes, and
women, too, into active persecution and unlawful
deeds.

This was the method that the stranger had
adopted in order to get his revenge upon Pan Andrew, and not only revenge, but that which he
sought even more keenly, the possession of the
pumpkin that the country gentleman had refused to
deliver to him early in the day. He had been about
the city seeking out certain friends or followers in
order to raise the cry of wizard, and then he had
with them searched through the city until they
came upon Pan Andrew and his wife.

"The pumpkin, the pumpkin—it is my brother's
head," he kept shouting.

Pan Andrew, on his side, only smiled back de-
risively upon him, and gathered in the pumpkin
where no man could seize it without taking as well

a blow from his heavy sword, and the attackers, being more cowards than men, made no attempt to approach the wagon at the side that he was facing. Some, armed with large stones, were, however, sneaking around to get behind him, and others in front were preparing to send a volley of missiles upon him, when there rushed into the turmoil a man of venerable appearance, clad in a brown robe with large puffy sleeves and pointed hood. He was of moderate stature, firm of gait, and bore himself like a man in the prime of life.

A priest he might have been, a brother of some order he seemed, but a scholar he was certainly, for there was that in his face and a droop to the shoulders that proclaimed him a man of letters.

"Cease—cease—cowards all!" he shouted in a commanding tone of voice. "What persecution goes on here?"

"The man and the woman and boy are workers in magic, wizards and a witch," said the leader roughly. "Keep your hands off, for we are admonishing them."

"Wizards and witches—fiddlesticks!" shouted the newcomer, pulling himself up in the wagon until he stood beside Pan Andrew. "This is but an excuse for some such deed of violence as this city has seen too much of in the past twelve months. To attack an honest man—for to any but a blind man he appears as honest—a weak woman, and a defenseless boy—Cowards all, I say! Disperse, or I will call the king's guards to disperse you."

"It is Jan Kanty himself," said one of the rioters in a loud whisper that all about him heard. "I'm off, for one." And throwing his stick to the ground, he took to his heels.

If there had been no magic in Pan Andrew, his wife, or his boy, there was magic in the name of Jan Kanty, and a very healthy magic, too, for at once every hat in that crowd came off, and men began to look askance at each other as if caught in some shameful thing.

"The good Jan Kanty," was whispered on every side, and in the briefest second imaginable the crowd had melted until there remained not one person, not even the leader of the ruffians who had begun the attack.

4

The Good Jan Kanty

Among the most remarkable personages of Krakow's age of glory in the fifteenth century was a certain scholar-priest by the name of Jan Kanty. He had been educated at the University of Krakow in the period of late Scholasticism when the chief teachings were still mere expositions of the seven arts, of which grammar was the king. However, a full life and much contact with men had made Jan Kanty a well-rounded man. He loved learning for its own sake, but he honored most of all its precepts and its application to life, and he gave himself over in his cell-like quarters on the lower floor of the old university building (now long since destroyed by fire), to the creation of new points of view on old subjects, to comments on the conduct and opinions of the masters and doctors of the university at the great church councils of Europe, and to an intellectual chronicle of his age.

His life was saintly and his cell was as much visited, perhaps, as is his shrine in the magnificent old university library today. The peasants loved him especially, and this was rather curious since the men from the farms rarely sought the advice of the men of the university; they were, in fact, somewhat shy of the dispensers of higher learning. They were not shy of Jan Kanty, however. They came to Krakow to ask his opinion on the weather in the seasons of grains and vegetables, they called upon him for decisions in disputes between landowners, they consulted him concerning the proper kind of food for their livestock, they questioned him on all problems having to do with morals or religion, and they accepted his rulings with as much finality and satisfaction as if they had been the rulings of Heaven.

Therefore his name was one to be reckoned with everywhere, inside the city and out. He hated above all things cruelty of man against man, or of man against something helpless, a horse, or a dog, or a child. And when he saw one man and a woman and a boy of honest features and good appearance harassed by some hundred men, he did not hesitate but rushed into the midst of the flying stones without regard to his own safety or comfort.

"Peace be with you," he said to Pan Andrew when the crowd had scattered, "and with you, my daughter," putting his hand upon the woman's head. "What may be the cause of such mischance? You are strangers here?"

"Strangers and worse. Homeless," said Pan Andrew.

"You are come from a long distance?"

"The Ukraine."

The kind shoulders rocked in agitation. "My—my—but surely you have friends in town?"

"I have none. I had a friend here and sought him, but he is dead. My house is burned by Tartars, my wealth is gone. I am pursued by men who seek my life and the one possession that I have left." Here he touched the pumpkin with his foot.

"But why this accusation of magic?"

Pan Andrew smiled. "A trick it was to raise feelings against me in the public square and then to despoil me of this possession. I think that he who raised the storm against me here has followed me many miles across the border, and I believe that he is the agent of some more powerful person. There is much to this, my good—my good—You are a priest?"

"Men call me so. I am but a servant of the Father of us all."

"Then, good father, hear me! I seek to do no man wrong. I am helpless in a world of plotting and troubles, and I seek only a place where I may this night provide shelter for my good wife and my boy."

"Come with me then," said the scholar-priest. "I will at least offer you the hospitality that my cell affords. . . . Nay—hitch your horses to the wagon and drive through that lane yonder which leads to the Street of St. Ann."

Pan Andrew was already adjusting the harness when Joseph tugged at his sleeve. "Father," he urged, "Father, I know of a place where we can stay."

The father looked down at him in astonishment. "You," he answered, "you? And how did you find such a place?"

"A scholar and his niece live there. They took me to their house. There is a space below them at the head of a flight of stairs."

Jan Kanty interposed. "Come at any rate to my dwelling, and there we can make plans. If the boy has found a place, and his face and words seem truthful, then we can talk at better length there at our ease than here in the busy square."

A few minutes later they stopped in front of the largest of a number of buildings which made up the university. On the way there Joseph had noted that almost every man they passed on the street had doffed his hat to Jan Kanty, and once a whole company of knights had saluted him with drawn swords. He seemed to pay but little attention to these courtesies, however, for his mind was busy with the problem of the present, and when he alighted from the cart and led the three to his little cell on the ground floor just at the right of the door, he was still pondering.

Once inside the house, however, Pan Andrew, disregarding Joseph's information for the minute, begged an immediate audience with Jan Kanty alone, and while the boy and his mother were eating some food which the scholar had placed upon a table in the corridor just outside his cell, he began to address his host in a low tone.

Their voices buzzed as Joseph and his mother ate. Only once did the boy catch distinct syllables, and that was when the priest asked Pan Andrew,

"That, then, is the pumpkin that you have brought from the Ukraine?"

Pan Andrew must have nodded, for he made no verbal answer. He had not dropped the precious vegetable from his hands during the entire conversation. Joseph heard no more of the talk, for he began at that moment to tell his mother of his own adventures of the morning.

As he progressed with his story she ceased eating and stared at him. "Why, this is a very miracle," she said. "As soon as Pan Andrew has finished with the good father in the next room, we will go straight about procuring the lodging of which the scholar told you. . . . And the poor child—she lost her father and mother in the plague? Indeed, I think that God must have sent us to her."

Jan Kanty at the farther end of the cell listened to Pan Andrew's tale to the very end. He asked a few questions, which the other answered, and then the two began to converse rapidly though in low tones.

At length Jan Kanty passed his hand across his eyes as if thinking very deeply. Then he said, "It seems to me that there is one course open to you. You have enemies in the city, you believe, and therefore you must remain for the present unseen. I advise a change of name, for such subterfuge is no sin where the end to be gained is righteous. For your present needs you can obtain money by selling your horses and cart; if you wish, I will send a man with them to the horse market in the plain below the Wawel. They would be but an encumbrance to you at best, and moreover they will bring a pretty price since they are of good stock and well fed."

"This money will not last me forever," said Pan Andrew. "I must think of some employment besides."

"I have thought of that," continued Jan Kanty. "I know of employment which might suit your case even though it be a humble task."

"It cannot be too humble for me," answered the other quickly, "provided it brings enough return for the support of my wife and boy."

"Good! Excellent!" exclaimed the scholar. "Then I have just the thing. You were a hunter in the old days, I presume?"

"Why, yes," said Pan Andrew, wondering.

"And you can sound the horn?"

"That I can. And if I do say it, with more skill than any hunter in the Eastern Marches."

"Good! . . . But yet one thing. This news which you have imparted to me should be for the ears of the king alone. The treasure which you guard should be returned to him, it should become the property of the commonwealth. I know not what harm it has already done in the world; I only hope that it may do no more. Would you leave it with me for safekeeping, perhaps?"

"Would that I could. But it was the oath that I took to my father that it should never leave my hands while life remained—save to one person, and that person the king of Poland."

"Then God be with you. Rest here until the

horses are sold and then after hearing your son's story we will think of tomorrow."

He called the mother and boy into his cell. "Why, here," he said on hearing the story of Joseph's adventure from his mother's lips, "is the thing arranged to perfection. I know the place you mention and I know the scholar Kreutz as well. A curious man, and of certain strange disposition, but honest and sincere and a seeker after light. He is, I think, feared by the common people, as are also many dwellers in the next street, which has been since olden times inhabited by sorcerers and their ilk, and the court of his house is but little frequented. They tell strange tales of him, sometimes, most of which I know to be false. But it is just the place for your dwelling at present, since there is little likelihood of your being disturbed there."

At this so great a feeling of thankfulness came upon Joseph's mother that she would have fallen to her knees and asked the good father for his blessing, but he restrained her.

"Nay, daughter," he said, "it is I who need thy blessing, since I know what fortitude and courage thy kind heart possesses."

She kissed his hand nevertheless, as did Joseph immediately afterward, and Pan Andrew turned away quickly lest they should see that his eyes were moist, for there is such power in kindness well bestowed that it touches the wells of human feeling. There was, too, something in this scholar-priest that went at once to the heart, some fine quality of feeling and spirituality that set him apart, though ever so sweetly and gently, from other men.

A servant of the university was dispatched to sell the horses and cart, and Joseph with his father and mother sat down to await the man's return.

While they were waiting, there came a knocking upon the outside door. Jan Kanty went to it at once. A woman stood there, with a baby in her arms, not in the attitude of one asking for alms but of one seeking advice. She came, it seemed, from the Black Village and was suffering much from pains that took her legs and arms and neck.

Jan Kanty questioned her quietly. "Where do you sleep?" he asked.

"On the floor, reverend sir," she answered. "And the aches and pains are so strong that I can stand them no longer. It is certain that a devil possesses me, and I would that you should pray him away."

"Is the floor made of stones?"

"It is."

"Are the stones ever wet?"

"No, reverend sir, except in spring."

"Is the earth damp beneath the stones?"

"Why—yes—perhaps," she said. "Sometimes when the well water is not much used it overflows, for there is a source there, and sometimes when they have been drawing water carelessly the overflow leaks down beneath the stones."

"Then take heed to what I say and the aches and pains will pass. Take stones and build a low wall between the well and the side of your cottage.

Make this waterproof and then dig a drain that will carry the water away from your house. Hang your bedclothes often in the sun and be sure that they are always dry. Change every week the boughs upon which you lie; thus will the pains go away."

She kissed his hand and departed.

Then came a peasant who complained that worms were coming up from the ground and were destroying the young shoots of his plants.

"Could you but say a prayer, father," the man supplicated, "the worms will cease."

"It is for you to prevent them," said Jan Kanty. "Sprinkle all the earth about the plants with ashes which you take from your stove. If this does not prevent the worms, then rise early in the morning and pour water about the plants. The worms will then come to the top where the water is, and you may kill them."

Then stooping over a high desk he began to write upon a long scroll of parchment, the end of which hung far over the desk almost to the floor. He used for writing the quill of a pigeon thrust into a piece of oak wood.

Joseph curled up on a bench that ran along beneath the windows and closed his eyes. What a day it had been! And what might the future hold?

His thoughts, which at first had begun to run slowly, suddenly became brisk and grew fantastic. He seemed to see himself bearing armor, a shield, and a sword, fighting desperately with a great dark-browed Tartar who had instead of a head a huge yellow pumpkin. Then the Tartar suddenly took off his head, and carrying it in his arms, climbed up a steep ladder to a room that seemed to hang from the stars. Out of it came lightning and flashes of strangely colored light, and suddenly the Tartar emerged, now with the head of a dog, and the pumpkin floating along beside him as if it were but a ball of feathers in the wind. The scratching of Jan Kanty's quill grew fainter and fainter, and the fantastic world dimmed slowly in blackness.

Joseph was fast asleep.

When he awoke the room was no longer filled with sunshine. A single candle lantern was burning at the farther end of the cell, and by its light he could see his father, Jan Kanty, and his mother busied with something that lay in front of them upon the table. He rubbed his eyes to make sure that he was awake—yes, it was the mysterious pumpkin, from which his father was slicing away the outer rind with a huge knife. It was a curious pumpkin, that vegetable—the rind was so hard and brittle that the knife scraped on it as if it were cutting or whittling away a piece of board. Joseph, fascinated, watched the process, almost afraid to breathe. Little by little the hard pieces dropped to the floor like bits of shell as the blade cut them through.

"I think," the father was saying in a low voice, "that I hold here in my hand the reason for the attack on my house in the Ukraine, and that the man who has hounded us today knew very well what this pumpkin shell contained. He had been told that I had it in my possession; he knew the exact size of my property, and he quickly put two and two together when he saw this pumpkin, and only this pumpkin, in my wagon. The reason that I made no effort to conceal it was, of course, to allay any suspicion concerning it."

"But," interrupted Jan Kanty, "a pumpkin at this time of year is likely to create some curiosity among those who give the matter a second thought. This is a late pumpkin, and I suppose that in all Poland it would be hard to find another such in midsummer."

"True," replied Pan Andrew, "but I had to risk that. Long ago when I was worried over this sacred charge and feared lest some enemy might discover its existence and attempt to rob me, there came to me the idea of a shell like this as an excellent means of concealment. Since that day there has never been a time, summer or winter, when there was not a pumpkin shell in readiness for an emergency, and many an experiment was I obliged to make, indeed, before I was able to preserve a shell in the good condition of this one."

At this moment he cut away the last piece of the rind.

The room was suddenly filled with the light of a thousand candles. Colors of the rainbow fell upon the walls—a huge center of radiance like the sun in the heavens blazed into being at the very place where the pumpkin shell had been but a moment before. Flickering, dancing flecks of light leaped about the room and transformed its gloom into the brilliancy of day—and then there was again but the light of the little lantern, for the father had placed that which the pumpkin contained in a bag furnished by Jan Kanty, and was busy tying up the open side when Joseph came rushing up to the table.

"Father," he cried, "what was it? What was the light which came from that which you took from the pumpkin?"

The father's voice was kindly but firm. "In time, Joseph, you shall know. It would be but a care to you, a matter of more worry than you suspect, if you knew what responsibility we are carrying here. If it is mere curiosity, be assured that knowledge will bring nothing but pain. If it is real interest, I will tell you plainly that in due time you shall be informed of all that has passed. Just now—it has cost me so much that I have not the heart to burden your young life with its secrets."

He broke off, and after a short silence, changed the subject.

"We will go now to that place which you have found for us. While you slept the reverend father and I have been to see your friends. He has seen to it that the rooms have been made comfortable, and there we shall stay, at least for the present."

5

In the Street of the Pigeons

St. Ann's Street was as black as pitch when they
emerged from the habitation of the scholar-priest.
He insisted on accompanying them and carried his
little candle lantern for aid, which, though it threw
a faint light upon the ground a step or two ahead,
yet had not much more light than the stars which
shone down from a moonless sky. Pan Andrew,
with his wife on his right arm, followed Jan Kanty,
and Joseph brought up the rear. They had taken
but a few steps along the narrow footwalk by the
side of the road when something damp and clammy
was forced into the boy's right hand; he gave a
little startled jump, but reassured himself at the
next minute that it was nothing but the nose of
a stray dog that had sought his hand as a token of
friendly greeting.

And as I live, thought Joseph as he reached
down and felt a great shaggy head, it's like the wolf
dog that leaped at Elzbietka this very day. Yes—
it's about the same size—and here: the collar is
exactly the same that I had my fingers through. I

know its feel by those little knobs that almost tear the flesh. "Father! Father!" he called.

Pan Andrew turned about quickly. "What is it?"

"A dog," answered the boy, "a friendly dog."

"Bring him along with us," said the father with a laugh, "we can't have too many friends just now." And at that they continued on their way.

Now of all the creatures that God has put in the world a dog is the most curious, and sometimes, one might think, the most discerning. For when this same animal had broken loose in the morning, his first impulse, which he had followed, had been that of flight. His second impulse was to look for a friend, since no dog can live without a friend. The Tartar boy had already departed. The dog had seen too much of him as it was. Also by virtue of a rare instinct which dogs, and sometimes horses, possess, the wolf dog had realized fully that the boy who had leaped at his collar was not an enemy. Perhaps it was the boy's touch, perhaps it was some quality in the tone of his voice, but the animal knew that Joseph was used to dogs and knew as well that he was just in his treatment of them. Therefore he had searched all day throughout the city streets, and when he came upon this little group of people in the dark street his sense of smell told him that here was a dog lover, and marvel of marvels, it was the same dog lover that had sprung upon him earlier in the day!

They turned at length from St. Ann's Street into a side lane that is known today as Jagiellonska, and followed it for a short distance until they reached the Street of the Pigeons. Here they turned to the left and walked for a few steps until suddenly just before them rose a babel of subdued voices. Father Jan Kanty stood stock-still. The others also came to a halt and remained motionless, except for the dog, which strained at Joseph's hold upon his collar.

"Stay," said the scholar. "I will go forward to see what may be in the air." And holding his lantern at the height of his head, he plunged into a crowd of black-robed figures that had formed a circle in the very middle of the street.

"Students," he cried aloud, as he swung his lantern first to this face and then to that, "students. And what devilment make you here now?"

The crowd broke before him at a touch. Either he was much feared by them or greatly respected —that Pan Andrew could see—perhaps both.

"A duel," he exclaimed as he reached the center of the crowd, where a space lighted by a lantern upon the ground had previously been obscured by the bodies of the lookers-on, "and what means it?"

Two young men, both students, with their black university robes lying beside them on the ground, stood facing each other with unfastened underjackets. Slender Italian dueling swords, or foils, held firmly in the clasped fingers of their bared right arms, had clashed the instant before Jan Kanty entered the arena.

"A duel," he repeated. "Do you not know that dueling has been forbidden I know not how many times within these streets bounding the university? Do you not know that it is punishable by fine or imprisonment even, if the duelers are students?"

His hands groped fearlessly for the weapons. "This is no play duel," he cried, as he gathered them in.

Indeed it was not! The young men were fighting with naked rapiers! In most of the students' duels the points of the weapons were capped with buttons to make them less dangerous, or if the engagements were to be with broadswords, the opponents wore breastplates and heavy gauntlets and helmets. But here stood two young men without a single precaution against injury, and it was quite evident that one of them would have been badly wounded had not the scholar brought the fight to an end.

"What means this?" he repeated. "Who may you be?"

Holding the lantern close up to the face of the nearer, he cried out suddenly in astonishment. "Johann Tring! As much would I have thought of seeing you here as I would have of seeing our own lord cardinal. You whom I thought more a slave to a crucible than to a sword. And your name?" he thundered at the other.

"Conrad Mlynarki of Mazovia," answered the student, thrusting his weapon back into his girdle and letting his eyes drop for shame.

"A Mazovian! Well, it rejoices me that you are ashamed, and there was perhaps reason for your anger, since I hear that Mazovians are insulted without much thought these days. Go to your room! I will hear your story tomorrow. And you" —he turned to the remnants of the original crowd, those few who remained, maliciously hoping to see punishment meted out to the offenders—"betake yourselves to your bursars with all possible speed, for if I see one of you here when I return, I will notify the authorities in the morning."

"As to you, Johann Tring," he addressed the other student when he stood alone with him in the middle of the street, "are you not ashamed at such a public brawl?"

"I am not," said the student quickly and without flinching at the look which Jan Kanty gave him.

At this moment Pan Andrew and the others came up to them. In the light of the lantern Joseph glanced at the face of the student, Johann Tring, and received almost a shock—a feeling at least of violent repulsion. It was not that the face was distorted, indeed it was not, the eyes were bright and piercing, and the hair was black—the carriage of the body was erect, and the whiteness of the skin where the collar was rolled back stood in re-markable contrast to the hair and the blackness that lay about him. But the nose was thin and mean, the mouth was small and smug, and out of the eyes came a look that signified an utterly selfish spirit behind them. For one so young this expres-sion was strange, and even more than strange; it was unnatural, and this unnaturalness was more apparent, even, to a boy of Joseph's age than it might have been to an older and maturer man who was used to much selfishness and meanness in the world.

"Now what caused this quarrel?" Joseph heard the scholar ask the question rather sharply.

"It is too long to tell at once—"

"Yes, but briefly."

"He insulted me."

"What did he say?"

"More things than one, but chiefly chided me about my studies. Asked me if I had learned yet how to make gold out of iron or brass or leather and said that he would collect old shoes all over the city if I would transmute them into precious metal."

"And this upon no provocation?"

The young man hesitated, yet there was something compelling about Jan Kanty that caused men to speak the truth to him. "I did ask him if the frogs in the north country spoke Mazovian," he answered in a rather sour voice.

"Yes, and I thought it was something like this," spoke Jan Kanty quickly. "Why must one always aggravate these Mazovians to their swords? I warn you here and now that, swordsman though you may be, the Mazovians are much more nimble with blades than with tongue."

"But he said further," went on Tring in self-justification, and being unable to express himself clearly in Polish, continued in German, much to Joseph's distress, for he could not understand a word.

"Have more caution, Tring," said the scholar at length. "Since you are not enrolled as a regular student of the university you must be even more careful in your conduct than if you were. . . . Since it is you who have first drawn your weapon, it must be you who make peace. Go tomorrow at dawn and kiss your opponent upon the cheek and sue him for pardon."

This advice sat hard upon Tring's temper, but he was so much influenced by the scholar that he finally bowed his head in consent.

"And further than this I might say, Johann Tring, that such occurrences bring you no credit. I know not much of your studies these days, though I think sometimes that you keep company more with necromancers and astrologers of little merit than with such worthy men as Pan Kreutz and his equals. These are dark days when men look with suspicion upon all who engage in investigation whether it be honest or dishonorable, godly or selfish. Are you still at Kreutz's?"

"I am."

"Then come with us, since we are bound for his dwelling. This Pan and his wife are taking the rooms below Kreutz's."

The young man tried to peer into the darkness beyond the lantern light to see who the new tenants might be, but none of the Charnetskis was visible.

They walked ahead a few steps until they came to the door where Joseph had been in the afternoon. Jan Kanty reached up and pulled the wire which hung down from above the door, and in a few minutes an old bent woman with a lantern scrutinized their faces from the open doorway and admitted them.

"All will be well now," said Joseph's father. "We need not trouble you further."

"It has been otherwise than trouble," protested

the scholar. "You will be well and comfortable, I am sure, for all the arrangements have been made. Tomorrow I shall send you the man who will tell you of your new duties. And now good night to you, Pan Andrew—Kovalski"—he hesitated a bit over the assumed name—"and may peace be with you."

"And with you." They all repeated it.

The kindly figure of the gentle, loving, saintly old man passed out into the darkness again. The woman slammed the door and bolted it heavily when the Charnetskis—now the Kovalskis—Johann Tring, and the dog were inside.

"At last," said Pan Andrew, "we are at home."

They passed through the passage with its pointed arches and emerged into the court, the woman leading the way with her lantern. Here Tring bade them good night and went to his room on the right-hand side of the court. Joseph felt at parting from him something of the same dislike that he had experienced when the lantern light had fallen upon his face in the street; the face was one that might easily come to haunt a man in his dreams, and yet it was in daylight but an ordinary face, like that of a thousand other students who possessed neither the gift of beauty nor the curse of ugliness—yet in that yellow gleam of the lantern there had been upon the features some indefinable threat of malignity.

The woman led them to the stairway on the left. As they ascended these same stairs that Joseph had climbed earlier in the day, the whole staircase seemed even more shaky and rickety than it had appeared in the light of day. The woman moved ahead of them freely, but Pan Andrew and his wife and Joseph clung to the railing as if for protection in case the boards should fall away beneath their feet.

At the first landing the door stood open. Out from this door came the welcome beam of a candle, lighted by the hands of Elzbietka Kreutz. The father with this candle in his hand at once inspected the little quarters. There were but two rooms, one of them fortunately large and of good shape, so that while one end of it must serve as a bedroom for Pan Andrew and his wife, there was ample room at the other end for the general living quarters of the family. The smaller room at the back Joseph would sleep in. The woman who had opened the door had been busy all the evening preparing the place for occupancy, expending some of the money which Pan Andrew had given her for bare necessities, a rug, wooden eating utensils, chairs, and beds.

He had left his name as Andrew Kovalski with the woman, the name which had been agreed upon with Jan Kanty, a name in itself one of the most common, since it signified a smith—and the alchemist and his niece, having been advised of the kinship with the Tenczynskis, willingly pledged silence concerning the true name.

"Well, wife," said Pan Andrew when they were alone and the door fastened, "this is better than we dared hope." Thereupon he laid down upon the table in the large room the precious round parcel which had not left his hands at any time since they had set out from Jan Kanty's cell. "Best of all we are safe here; the door is heavy, the front of the building is of stone, and from the rear no one could climb over the wall without danger to himself. It is, indeed, the wall of a monastery to which none but monks have access. Above us is the alchemist Kreutz, and below on the ground floor are the old woman and her son, both of whom take care of the building and watch the gate at night.

"Across the way live a few students; one of them this Johann Tring who accompanied us. Those seeking us would never think of looking for us here; the change in name is also a protection. Here we may stay in comfort until such time as we may communicate with the king."

He intended to say more, but was interrupted by a curious sound that came from outside, as if a heavy body were dragging itself along. The mother uttered a little cry of fear; Pan Andrew reached for the handle of his short sword, but Joseph broke into a laugh.

"It is my dog rubbing against the door," he said. "He is tired and hungry, and no doubt wants a little water. There is a well in the court below from which I will draw it, and he can sleep then in the shelter of the wall. Tomorrow I must procure a chain or rope to fasten him with, for he is nearly wild and might cause trouble if he ran about." With this, Joseph searched in a basket for a bit of meat and a piece of bread, and finding them, descended to the court below. It was dark there but his mother held the lantern above him so that he could see to draw water and settle the dog in a corner of the wall.

When they returned his father was preparing for bed. The valuable package had been disposed of somewhere; with curious eyes Joseph scanned every inch of the large room and came to the conclusion that the only hiding place in the quarters was that afforded by the bed, either in the shadowy place beneath it, or somewhere in the bedding or folded clothes beneath the headrest.

He ceased to wonder very long about it, however, for his eyelids were heavy, despite his sleep of the afternoon. The whole world drifted off into oblivion, it seemed, the minute that he laid his head on the stuffed bag that served for a pillow.

The next day all were astir early. The mother was at work polishing the woodwork, and the father was driving nails to strengthen the cheap chairs, or covering cracks in the wall, and later inspecting the old staircase outside the building to see if he might mend it. The daylight inspection brought with it some satisfaction, for while it confirmed his belief that the staircase was shaky, yet it revealed that the underpinnings were firmer than might be supposed. The staircase might last for some years if it did not have rough usage, and certainly there was no immediate danger, as Pan Andrew had feared the night before.

Joseph took an early opportunity, after he had eaten the breakfast brought by the old woman who lived below, to run forth into the Street of the Pigeons with the dog, whom he named at once Wolf. In the daytime the street wore little of the sinister aspect that it carried at night; the little oval windows that had seemed then like wicked eyes peering down, now were more like the eyes of merry gnomes or pixies. The buildings which in the twilight, or even in the nighttime when lights fell upon them, seemed grotesque or terrible, in the light of day seemed only curiously twisted out of shape and hung out and bent inward in every conceivable fashion. All the lower windows bore heavy iron bars; doors carried great metal hinges that spread like trees over the surface of the hard wood, and chains dangled and rattled when the house occupants went in or out. From some windows hung clothes—women's clothing, long hose worn by men, jackets, and here and there, a student's black gown. The novelty of the street attracted the boy, and for a long time he wandered through it curiously.

At the upper end, where it met a cross street that ran toward the Rynek, the Street of the Pigeons curved quite sharply. Joseph finally ran with the dog clear to this cross street, which bore the name Bracka, and then, retracing his steps, bore back to the house which had now become his home. Mounting the steps rather breathlessly, he threw open the door to the outer room and was about to shout a merry greeting, as was his usual custom, but checked himself at sight of a stranger who stood talking with his father. The newcomer, who had a pleasant face, was dressed in leathers somewhat like those of the night watch when the outer chain armor is removed. On the table in front of the men lay a long brass trumpet, made cunningly and polished until it resembled gold.

By the side of the trumpet lay two parchment

scripts, one of them evidently a copy of a long piece of writing, the other—as Joseph could see— a set of musical notes worked carefully in red and black.

"This," said the stranger, pointing first to the script containing the writing, "is a copy of the oath that you have already sworn. This other is the music of the Heynal, the hymn which you must play from the church tower every hour of the night. The trumpeter whom you relieve tonight will give you the key to the tower room, and what information you may need. It is a noble piece of work, this sounding of the Heynal, and I am much pleased that Father Jan has been able to find so good a Pole as you to carry out the night duties." With this, he kissed Pan Andrew upon the right cheek and departed.

Joseph stared in frank amazement. The Heynal! The church tower. And his father!

"I will tell you everything," said the father as they sat down to the noonday meal. "This oath which I have sworn is the customary oath taken by the watchman-trumpeter of the tower of the Church of Our Lady Mary. You may read it at your leisure. The music is the hymn with the broken note of which I have promised to tell you the story soon. It is played each hour from the windows in the octagon room at the top of the higher tower."

"And you are to be the trumpeter?" asked Joseph.

"I am, thanks to the good Jan Kanty," the father answered. "The trumpeter and the watchman as well, for it is from this tower that fires throughout the city are sighted and the alarm given with the big bell. For the present it must be for our own safety that we are known as the Kovalski family, a name which Father Jan has given us. As plain Andrew Kovalski I shall be a mere city dweller of Krakow. I shall be trumpeter, succeeding the man—God rest his soul!—who died but a week ago, since which time there has been a substitute who can play but badly."

"But the man said each hour of the night," exclaimed the boy. "Will you be there all night?"

"Yes," answered Pan Andrew. "It is for my own safety to be abroad in the city only after nightfall. None will recognize me then—and as for you, my son, the good father has arranged that you shall attend the Collegium Minus here, to complete your studies, which I and your tutors have already begun with you. But there must be caution employed even by you, for there are people who seek nothing better than to find us and despoil us of our treasure. You may take your exercises with the other boys very soon, however, and go abroad with discretion, for in the clothes which I shall buy you there will be no danger, I think, that you may be recognized. A close mouth is necessary nevertheless. Tell no one of our adventures and be content for the time with the plain name Joseph Kovalski."

Thus, at the direction of the good Jan Kanty, Pan Andrew became Pan Kovalski—Joseph was to be sent to school—and the watchtower of the Church of Our Lady Mary was to see a new trumpeter.

At the moment that the father had ceased speaking, there came running into the room from the staircase the girl Elzbietka Kreutz, who made straight for Joseph's mother and was caught into her arms. "We shall be happy here," the woman exclaimed, "that I know, and here is one that needs a mother's love." The girl turned to smile to Pan Andrew, whose face grew gentle at the sight of her eyes, and he picked up her slim, dainty hand and kissed it—it was indeed a picture, that fragile white hand lying in his huge brown palm.

"Uncle has told me," she said, "that you are to play the trumpet at the church. Often at night, when I lie awake lonely and have strange fears, I listen for the music from the steeple. And now when I know that it is Joseph's father that is playing I shall go to sleep again and fear nothing."

"It is as if I had two children," said Pan Andrew, slipping one arm about the child and the other about his son. "It truly seems as if God has once more smiled upon us."

6

The Tower
of the Trumpeter

One of the great sights of central Europe, even in those faraway days, which men came from all parts of the world to see, was the Church of Our Lady Mary in Krakow. Now, though this church rose majestically over the medieval city, its towers visible from afar, and its red brick walls as substantial and as solid as the very rock base of the Wawel Hill itself, it was not from the outside such as imposing sight as was its more aristocratic sister, the Wawel Cathedral. It lacked flying buttresses and distinct Gothic ornamentation, such as huge gargoyles and flowers and saints carved in stone, though its graceful form indicated a solid and magnificent strength. It was not a church such as one might gaze upon in sunny France, where the mild breezes and sweet sunshine permit delicate carvings and pinnacles upon the outside walls, but it was built like a solid fortress to withstand the mighty storms that sometimes sweep over Poland from the wild steppes or from the Baltic Sea. It was the interior of this church, however, that drew men to it, for within, it was a very miracle of beauty, a crystal hidden in a shapely stone.

It was to this church, then, that Pan Andrew and Joseph wended their way after darkness fell on their first day in the new dwelling. Pan Andrew carried the trumpet under his right arm. Near the base of the higher tower a watchman spied them as they approached, and unlocked a small, heavy door that led to the tower stairs. They went up a narrow staircase, winding about in the darkness, until it reached a platform where the interior of the tower loomed suddenly above them. Just at the right, as they began their ascent in the main body of the tower, was a door that led to a little chapel in which, as Joseph learned afterward, prisoners condemned to death spent their last hours on earth.

A man carrying a lantern shouted to them from above; they waited then until he had descended— he was the day watchman whom Pan Andrew relieved. He paused to kiss Pan Andrew upon the cheek in welcome, and to speak a few words in explanation of his duties above. Then he placed in his hand the lantern and a key to the room which the trumpeter was to occupy in the high tower. He wished them luck on their first night and then descended by the side staircase to the ground, where the watchman let him out. Joseph and his father in the meantime began to climb the steps of the scaffolding that led up into the tower. This scaffolding was held in place by crossbeams, and at its edge ran the steps, so built that as a man ascended he passed constantly from one of the four sides of the

tower to another side. The staircase was steep and
narrow, but very solid, so solid that the stairs did
not creak as they ascended.

They climbed and climbed, past five levels of
windows glassed in with small white globes of solid
crystal. Up and up went father and son, until they
reached the level where there was a room for the
watchman. This octagonal room was divided into
two sections, one being the room where the trumpeter might keep warm between watches, the other
being the open space around it, from which the
turret windows looked out over the city. Here hung
extra trumpets, here were the ropes which connected with the great bell hanging in the lower
tower, and here were the red flags and the lanterns
which were hung out when a fire was perceived
from the tower.

For it was the duty of the trumpeter to watch
constantly for fires. He was to watch also for
troops approaching the city, for tumults or dis-
turbances of any kind, but he was especially the
guardian against fires. Conflagrations had done the
city much harm in the past; many of the older
buildings were of wood, although fronted with
stone, and roofs were often of thatch or soft wood
that easily caught fire from sparks. When a fire was
discovered, the trumpeter or watchman, for he was
both, hung a red flag from the window which faced
the direction in which the blaze lay. At night he
would hang out a lantern with a red glass front
instead of the flag.

It was his duty also to sound the alarm bell if
any danger whatever came to threaten the lives of

citizens. In the very month previous to the coming
of Pan Andrew and his family to Krakow, the
watchman had rung loud and long upon the bell to
alarm the watch and the city when the riot against
the Tenczynski family took place. In the coming
year the bell was to be tolled at the execution, in
the town square just below the tower, of the four
men charged with causing the riot. The tower was
indeed the very center of Krakow activity.

Pan Andrew fitted his key to the lock of the
door leading into the inner room and threw back
the bolt. Entering after his father, Joseph found
himself in a small comfortable room containing a
table, a bed, a small stove, and a lighted lantern
hanging on the wall. About the table were three
chairs, wedged rather tightly because of the lack of
space, and upon the table was a huge hourglass,
one of the largest that Joseph had ever seen. The
sand pouring through it in a fine stream had filled
the lower section almost to a level graded on the
glass with a Latin "X" to designate the tenth hour.
The glass was in reality a twelve-hour glass, and
lines and Latin numerals had been marked upon it
just after the maker had blown it into shape, when
the material was still soft. This was the trumpeter's
official clock. There was on the south side of the
nave roof, where the sun touched at all hours of
the day, a large sundial which was read each noon,
and on the north wall of the tower was a clock
with one hand. This hand, which indicated the
hours, was in truth a hand—a piece of metal
shaped like a double fist—with fingers curled and
the index pointing out to the hours.

When the sand had reached the level of the glass at which the "X" was cut, Pan Andrew hastened out to the open section of the tower and released a coil of rope that hung on a pillar in the center of the space. This rope ran down through a hole in the flooring, until it reached the level of the lower tower, when it swung about over a piece of round wood that served as a pulley and leaped from there to the lower tower through an aperture that was originally designed as a narrow window through which to shoot arrows in time of defense. In the lower tower the rope was connected with one end of an iron hammer that was suspended above the great bell. When the rope was pulled the hammer descended, but it sprang quickly back to its original position when the rope was loosed, a spring of twisted metal and leather serving to draw it back. Pan Andrew pulled once—the hammer descended —boom—the stroke of the bell sounded over the whole city. He pulled again and again until the full quota of ten strokes was made.

Next he went to the side of the tower nearest the entrance to the little room and swung back a small glass window. Through this space he thrust the trumpet and began to play. It was on the west side, the side toward the Cloth Hall, with the university in the distance. Then he moved to another window but one and began to play toward the south. Likewise he played toward the east, and finally toward the north, according to the instructions which he had received. Lights were twinkling now all over the city below him; the air was soft and smelled of the freshly cut grass which the peasants gather into piles. In the direction of the university a group of men were chanting a hymn. A clashing of iron hoofs on the stones of Grodzka Street betokened the presence of some armed men, perhaps the servitors of some nobles' houses at the castle, or perhaps members of the royal guard. Men of the night watch could be heard banging at doors of shops with the butts of their spears to be sure that no careless apprentice or servant had left the door ajar. Down below, in the graveyard, the white stones were just perceptible, dim and gray in the dusk; and over the way, the lamplighter was enkindling the huge wicks of the lamps that hung under the Cloth Hall roof. The stars were coming out, one after another, in the sky, where a touch of blue still lingered—across this world rang the notes of the hymn which Pan Andrew had just played exquisitely, the Heynal, or Hymn to the Holy Mother.

"It is wondrous sweet," said Joseph.

"It is so, my son," replied the father. Thereupon he told the boy of the morning, years before, when the square below them had been full of hostile Tartars; of the lad who had kept his oath, even with the last breath of life itself; and of the honor paid him from that day to this by the tower trumpeters who end the Heynal at the broken note.

And Joseph, listening with eyes shining and heart throbbing, realized more at that moment than ever before how dear to him was his native land and all the customs that had been bequeathed by brave men and women who had made it great forever among all nations; it seemed as if tears were forcing themselves to his eyes as he thought of the sacrifice of that young life so many years before, but a thrill of pride drove back the tears when he thought of the nobility of the deed, as he stood silently gazing out of the little tower window.

They re-entered the inner room.

"I have brought you here tonight," Pan Andrew explained when he had closed the door and hung the trumpet on the wall, "in order to instruct you in the duties of the trumpeter of this church. For there might come a time when I should be ill, or perhaps even wounded—who knows, since I have so many enemies? I have taken the oath that I will play this trumpet each hour, and that it is no vain oath you have learned from the story which I have just told you. The trumpet must be played, happen what will. Therefore"—he drew out a piece of parchment and sketched on it with a bit of charcoal a series of lines—"you are to learn by heart the notes which I sketch here.

"Here are the notes of the Heynal," he continued after he had worked silently some minutes upon his composition, "the tune goes like this." He hummed the melody and indicated on the parchment how each symbol represented a note.

"This," he said, "it is necessary to learn. Work upon it during the coming week, and at this time next week be able to write it out. Do not let it interfere with your work at the collegium but glance at it in spare time. Also, if you can, sing to yourself beneath your breath the melody of the Heynal. When you have learned the melody, I will teach you to play it upon the trumpet. It is not a hard task, although perfection comes only after much effort. I will teach you single tongue and double tongue, and triple tongue, which is the queen of the trumpeter's music, just as grammar is king of the scholastic kingdom."

Joseph slipped the parchment inside his coat.

"And now," directed the father, "go down the stairs quickly and run with dispatch to our house. As you descend leave the lantern against the wall on the lowest tower level; be sure that you extinguish it. The mother is waiting and may be already lonely."

"Nay, I left her with Elzbietka."

"Bless the child. But, just the same, go with all speed, for city streets are dangerous at night. Keep close to the watchmen where possible, and if asked why you are out so late, reply that your father is trumpeter in the tower and that you are returning home with a message from him."

Joseph descended; he left the extinguished lantern at the place where the steps begin to mount the scaffolding and felt his way down the stone steps to the tower door. There he rapped, until the watchman let him out. Once in the street he was off like the wind, until he found himself in the Street of the Pigeons.

Much to his surprise the entrance door was opened, not by the old woman who saw to the care of the building, but by her son, who up to this time had kept himself well out of sight. As the light from the lantern fell upon his face, Joseph drew back in alarm; when his father had mentioned the fact that the old woman was living with her son,

Joseph had imagined that the son was a youth, or perhaps a boy—he did not expect to see a man who had the face of one of middle age. Yet the term "man" was less applicable to the son than was the word "creature," for he was lank and thin and bowed over uncannily; long wisps of hair fell about his eyes; his fingers were bony and clawlike; his cheeks were sunken, and his eyes peered out of hollow caverns as if they feared the light. As he moved ahead of Joseph, with the lantern in his hand, he clung to the wall as does a cat, shunning open spaces and skulking as if always needing a rear defense.

At the foot of the stairs he stopped.

Joseph was about to pass him and begin the ascent when the creature raised one of his hands and passed it over the boy's shoulder. Joseph heard the long nails scraping on his coat—in a horrible second it seemed as if he could feel them on his skin. The perspiration broke out on his forehead.

"What do you want?"

"A little—little coin," whispered the man.

Joseph handed him a piece of copper gladly.

"Good boy—good boy," the other mumbled, "bless thee, bless thee. And when you have much that jingles remember Stas. Stas I am, and here I sleep." He pointed at the door standing open on the lower floor, but Joseph's eyes did not follow him. His attention was taken suddenly from Stas by a burst of flame that leaped like a live thing from the tiny window of the loft of the alchemist on the fourth floor. It was just a little flare—a small flame that issued through the opened shutter, which the alchemist usually kept closed—it died down in a second or even less, but for that instant it lighted up the whole court and the surrounding buildings.

"Hey," said the man, pointing upward, "there they have magic that takes a soul away from a body. . . . See"—there was another flash, brighter than the first and longer continued—"there be devils that come to earth with the fire of hell upon them. . . . Their servant is the alchemist Kreutz, and they have one among us here on earth that is more like them than like us. . . . You know whom I mean?" He swung the lantern close to Joseph's face, the boy recoiling fearfully. "The student Tring! He it is that would deal with the devil and give him his soul. Have I not heard him at night as he lay awake in his room on the farther side of the court, mumbling and calling and singing? He it is who is the curse of this house. . . . Well, I must sleep. A good night to you." And he went in through the open door.

7

In the Alchemist's Loft

Joseph found himself too sleepy when he was inside his tiny bedroom to give any further attention either to the flashes of light from the loft above or to the mysterious grumblings of Stas. And the beginning of his studies at the Collegium Minus on the following day, drove, for the time being, all matters of lesser importance from his mind. There was an evening a week or more later, however, when the incident recurred to him. He had accompanied his father, as was his custom, to the tower, and returning early, had paused for a moment on the landing outside his door before entering the house. The night was fine and he peered contentedly about over the starlit roofs, the red chimneys, and the black walls. Down below him Wolf started uneasily in his sleep, as if he were dreaming of evil things. From the little window of the room beside the door of his own dwelling there was thrown upon the darkness a faint glimmer from a lamp which signified that his mother was sitting up, perhaps with Elzbietka, who had said earlier in the day that she would come down that evening.

He fell to musing in the sweet calm of the night, as young people will do, and in his musing wondered mightily what might be the importance which his father had attached to the treasure which he had brought to Krakow. It might be a gem worth thousands and thousands of gold zloty—it might be merely a fashioned piece of glass of value only to the tradesmen who worked in glass. But then, why had it made the impression that it had upon Jan Kanty, and why was the bold stranger so eager to gain possession of it? And why in such a peaceful world must names be changed and goings and comings veiled in a mantle of night? Why—

Flash! Into the night suddenly leaped the same brilliance that had startled him on that earlier evening when he had been alone in the court with Stas. Only, immediately following it now, here came a cry of someone in fright or pain.

The door at the landing above him was thrown open and a figure in white emerged. It began to descend the stairs hurriedly, and as it came near, Joseph saw that it was Elzbietka in her night clothes, over which she had thrown a white coverlid from her bed.

He spoke quickly in order that his presence might not alarm her.

"Elzbietka," he said, "it is I, Joseph. What has happened?"

"My uncle," she cried, "Joseph, I know not what they are doing."

"I thought you were with my mother," he exclaimed.

"I was, but I became sleepy, and she told me to go up and sleep. I did sleep, for some time, too. But then this loud talking and noise began. Joseph," she came close up to him, "Joseph, I am frightened. Something is going on upstairs that is not good. The student Tring is with my uncle always now. He came early in the evening, and they have been there together ever since. Uncle never used to go up there at night before—he stayed with me. Joseph, I fear that student Tring."

"I know what you feel," he said.

"I believe that he has some power over people that is not of this earth," she continued. "You do not know how much my uncle has changed since he first knew him. And I am all alone."

"What did you hear tonight?" asked the boy.

"I was awakened by a loud tramping on the floor. Then my uncle said, 'No, that will kill.' Then the student laughed a terrible laugh. After that there was a long, long silence. I was almost asleep again when I heard another voice—it was like to no one that I had ever heard before. There was something about it that made me think it was my uncle speaking, but it was in such a tone that it made my blood run cold. And now there are those flashes of light. Joseph, if you would serve me, climb the stairway and look through the casement. Do not let them see you, and do not stay long. Come down as soon as you can and tell me that my uncle is alive and well."

"I will. But first you go in and stay with Mother. You can sleep here tonight if you wish, and tomorrow I will ask my father what can be done."

He knocked at the door, but without waiting for his mother to come, ran up the second flight of stairs and reached out for the first board of the rude staircase. When he had found it he managed the ascent by clinging to the rail at the side, for the steps here were much steeper than those below; indeed, in the dark it seemed to him a dizzy bit of a climb, but he managed it nimbly and found when he reached the landing that he could just peep in through one corner of the opened window shutter. Had the shutter been closed, as it usually was, he could have seen nothing, for the glass, consisting of little round uneven blocks, was unglazed and set into a network of lead. Through the opening he peered, clinging to the railing of the stairs for support, and keeping one foot close to the top step, in order to descend in haste at the first hint that the occupants of the room were aware of the presence of a third person.

What he saw at first glance startled him, for the loft was literally blazing with light coming from oils burning in four copper braziers which hung from the ceiling. Above these braziers, to protect the roof from the heat, were layers of metal, one separated from the other, so that an air current played between them and cooled them. A fifth brazier, not now alight, hung close to the window where Joseph was peering, and it was from this brazier that the flame had sprung that had lighted up the whole court—as a matter of fact, the light had come from the rapid combustion of a handful of powder which the alchemist had thrown on the brazier's charcoal.

The loft itself was higher than the boy had realized—there was but one large room in it, for on the farther side could be seen the shutters of the building's outer wall. In the middle of the room at the back was a closet—for Pan Kreutz's most valuable substances, Joseph decided, since it was fastened with chains as well as with a huge lock and key. The beams of the roof, sloping but slightly, were well above the height of a tall man and were not of bare wood, as is common in lofts and attics, but were plastered over with some thick white substance.

In the center of the room stood a tripod supporting an iron basin, and in it was burning some substance that gave a peculiar pungent odor.

The alchemist in his black robe and the student Tring in his leather jacket sat elbow to elbow before this basin. They were watching something that was burning there in flames of many colors.

"It takes away my strength," Joseph heard the alchemist tell Tring, "to experiment in the fashion which you have suggested. It has interested me, and I know that it has its fascination, but it is not, after all, in my sphere. I am an alchemist, one who seeks the truth above all things in the actions and reactions of material substances. I mix vinegar and sugar and soda, and there is immediately a bubbling and a change. Something new is created. I melt lead and silver and copper, and they form together some metal that is new."

"But are not these changes influenced also by the position of the stars in heaven?" asked Tring.

"Yes, and no. The sea, I admit, seems to follow the pull of the moon. Harvests depend upon seasons and seasons sometimes seem to be servants of the movements of the heavenly bodies. But as to other things I know not. Besides, I am not an astrologer. I am an alchemist. The powers of the sky may be found by those who search the skies."

"But is not the conduct and life of man governed by the stars?"

"That I leave to magicians and necromancers, as likewise I leave to them that hideous magic which makes compounds of cats' paws, and owls' eyes, and dead men's fingers."

"But," persisted the student, "you seek the elixir of life, do you not?"

"No," answered the alchemist, "although in regard to it I admit that I have much curiosity. If it is true that all things are subject to change, then one might change from old to young as well as from young to old if one could but find the laws to reverse the process of life. And as to this I do not doubt that a restorer of youth can be found. Yet I am not interested as are those who have lived vain lives and hope to do better if life may be relived."

"The Philosophers' Stone, what think you of that?" Joseph noticed a distinct change in the student's voice as he said this; his eyes shone with a greedy light, and his fingers seemed to curl perceptibly.

"Well," answered the alchemist, "that is indeed much sought. To the superstitious and ignorant the

Philosophers' Stone means only some substance which by magical power can transform all things it touches into gold, like King Midas of ancient days. But to us who study and work, it is apparent that only a process and not a substance can bring this to pass."

"How—how?" demanded the student, leaning forward.

"Well, it is commonly known that each substance in the world, such as brass, or paper, or glass, has certain properties in itself. Did not Archimedes, father of all our learning, establish this truth by the proof that different substances thrown separately into water each displace a different amount of water? Gold is a substance, brass is a substance, both susceptible to change in the elementals, fire, water, air, and earth. Fire melts, water changes the color or disintegrates, air hardens, and earth darkens. To make brass of gold, or gold of brass is not impossible if one might know what would break down the dissimilarity between them."

"Then why do you not keep trying until you find the secret?"

The alchemist drew a long breath. "There are things that interest me more. Though I am an alchemist, I am much concerned with the spirit which is behind material things. I would learn if life itself is a matter of substance, if there is not the same difference between man and man that there is between metal and metal. I would learn the secrets of the earth, the messages of the sky, and I would know as well the secret of the soul, and how one might seek to help and save the souls of men whose bodies are from birth misshapen. I would learn, if I might, the composition of the earth, the reasons for the spring and summer and such phenomena—I would learn what makes the stars to shine and the sea to be tempestuous. God has given me a mind that searches ever for the light, and I feel that I am doing His will when I seek the truths that lie about us on every hand."

Tring came close and spoke very low, though his voice carried to Joseph at the casement.

"You are a fool, you, Pan Kreutz," he said. "Here are you, the most gifted scholar and alchemist of our time, fretting away your hours in such pursuits, with a much greater object to be gained at your very elbow."

"You mean—"

"You know what I mean. You and I have begun to experiment in things that men know but little of."

"I know, and I am of two minds about it. There is something in what you persuade me into that I like not. But upon such matters you are indeed the teacher and I the student. This I do know, and that is that when I am in a trance such as you sent me into a short time ago I can see things and hear things and even know things that I am not familiar with in my everyday mind. But such experiments, though they enthrall the soul, are perhaps dangerous to men. They are tried in Nuremberg, I believe, and in other lonely places in the Black Forest. But here in Krakow we have ever been wary of them."

The alchemist was looking into the fire. Tring, sitting beside him, cast at him at these words such a malicious look and leer that Joseph shuddered. There flashed into Joseph's mind the word "demon" —a veritable demon from the darkness Tring seemed, striving to exert some influence over his victim.

The look passed. "Pan Kreutz," began Tring again, "I know from my teachers in the old town of Nuremberg that man has in reality two brains. One of these brains is wise and powerful and dominant, and yet one knows nothing of it except when one is asleep in such a trance as I put you in but a short while ago. The other is the brain of daily life; by it we know when to eat, work, and rest. It is the lesser brain."

"Something of this you have proven to me," said the alchemist.

"Then use your higher brain," commanded Tring.

"To what end?" asked Kreutz.

"To the end that all men would reach. Gold!"

He said the word with an intensity that sent a cold thrill through Joseph.

"Gold matters not so much to me," answered the alchemist.

"It does—it does—it does," insisted Tring. "You do not know what you could do with it. With this secret, you and I could become the very kings of the earth. We could live in the finest palace in the world—we could have diamonds and rubies and emeralds—we could travel about the lands of Europe like the mightiest of merchant princes—

armies would be at our disposal, and we could make every human being perform our will."

For a moment he forgot the alchemist as he reveled in this dream made out of fancy and desire, but as a glance at Kreutz's face found no response there, he went on more cunningly:

"Think what you could do as an alchemist! Is this attic a fitting place for your experiments? Are these poor tools sufficient for the concoctions that you would devise and for the laws which you would prove? You could become the greatest alchemist in Poland—in the world! You could work in a room that would contain this poor attic a dozen times. In it would be every instrument that has ever been invented for the study of alchemy. No precious substance that comes out of the East, no priceless gem nor precious stone would be beyond the means that you would possess. Does this not tempt you?"

He had touched him this time. "It would tempt any poor scholar," Kreutz replied, in the voice of one who had seen a sudden vision. Then more keenly, "But do you think that I possess in myself, my greater self as you call it, this secret of changing base metals into gold?"

"I am sure of it"—Tring was almost dancing about his chair in eager enthusiasm—"if you will cease being a plodding scholar and a fool and set yourself night and day to conquer this problem of the universe. Gold—gold—gold—that is what every man wants. Success always means gold, and those who work all their lives professing none but unselfish motives are but deceiving others in order to make themselves reverenced—some of them perhaps are deceiving themselves. Why, with gold—think what you could do for your niece, think what you could do for the students of the university—you could make this school and, aye, the whole kingdom of Poland the greatest and most desired place in all the world."

Kreutz thought deeply for some minutes. It was quite evident even to Joseph, young and inexperienced as he was, that Tring had utterly poisoned the alchemist's mind. Indeed, now Kreutz, looking at life through the philosophy of Tring, saw that his own life was the life of a dusty plodder; it was the life not only of a poor man but of a foolish man who might be better off if he wished, who now had the opportunity to do a great deal for those whom he loved, if he would but set himself to it. His thoughts had been on a plane too high for practicality. He had idealized mankind and he had tried to learn things which had seemed to him to be the very jewels of knowledge in the crown of wisdom—yes, that was what he had been, a dusty old plodder.

And with these thoughts he surrendered utterly to Tring. "You are right, I truly believe," he said with a sigh. "Perhaps then we can possess this secret which will make us kings of the earth, as you say. With gold we can do these things, we can accomplish what we wish in the world, we can help the struggling, cure the sick, and do away with poverty entirely in this kingdom. Yes, it is, after all, a noble task—shall we repeat the experiment again tonight? Shall I enter into a trance again?"

"Nay," Tring had gained his end, "it is getting late and I would not repeat the experiment so shortly after the first trial, for fear perhaps that it would not be so successful as before. Tomorrow evening we shall try it, when we are both fresh again. . . . It was curious that tonight, when you were in the deepest part of the trance, you called out that that which every astrologer, alchemist, and magician has sought for centuries was within a few yards of the place where you sat. I had begun to think that we were upon the eve of a great discovery."

"Aye, it was then that something woke me," said the alchemist.

"Yes, the worse for us all," said Tring sourly. "It was a cry that brought you to your senses, upon the eve of so great a revelation. It was the cry of your niece from the room below."

"Elzbietka," exclaimed the alchemist with concern. "And why did she cry?"

"You were not silent in your trance. You shouted that there were some demons near by ready to kill you—you almost screamed in your fear—and then you talked as if your tongue were a pendulum."

"And I did not answer the child?"

"No. You sank back in your chair again, asleep, and this time it was a natural sleep, for when I questioned you again, you said nothing."

The alchemist rubbed his eyes. "I am sleepy now, in faith." Then, wondering, "What could have been the revelation? I know of no prize that could be near by. On the ground floor is the old woman, and her half-wit son, whom I frighten with fire—then on the second floor, but the three poor refugees installed recently. Across the court, only you and two poor students. No, it can be nothing in the possession of any one of these. Well, as you say, this for tonight is enough—" And at these words Joseph scampered down the stairway.

8

Peter of the Button Face

Summer burned itself into fall. The Vistula, which had been growing ever lower and lower with the heat, was now but a narrow ribbon of water, and the banks along it were parched and dried and yellow. Leaves were changing from green to brown, and the birds were making ready to leave for southern lands as soon as the first suggestion of cold should appear. Across the meadows now the horses and wagons were marching daily, and the dry hay was filling barn and shelter in all the country about. The fruits of the autumn were already appearing in the market, the apples of the first bearing, the golden squashes, and the late cabbage. And over the city and country hung a sky of deep, exquisite blue, for in all the world there is no sky so blue as is the Krakow sky, and no sun is so gold as is the sun of early autumn.

When the Month of the Heather had passed by and the Month of Hemp Beating was at hand, Joseph had learned all the notes of the Heynal and could play the little hymn upon his father's trumpet. Once even, he had played it in the tower; on that night his father had played it toward the west, south, and east, and then had allowed the boy to play it at the north window. The girl, Elzbietka, a little quicker of ear than Joseph, had long since mastered the air and quickly memorized Joseph's notes, so that she could not only hum the music, but reproduce it in writing upon a wall or piece of parchment.

One evening when Elzbietka was visiting Joseph's mother—and she came more and more frequently now, since the alchemist had began to carry on new experiments with Tring—Joseph exclaimed suddenly:

"Before long I shall play all four Heynals."

She let her chin rest upon one hand, as she did often when she thought and when she spoke seriously. "I shall listen," she said. "It comforts me more than ever now when I hear the hymn played in the nighttime—since there is seldom anyone in our rooms when I awake. Joseph," she spoke in a very low tone, "do you know I think that my uncle is possessed?"

He gave a great start. "Possessed—and by whom?"

"I don't know. But he isn't himself. It isn't that he is out of his wits—no, not that at all. He is just as intelligent and just as kind as he ever was, but he has become so interested in something that he is doing in the loft that he thinks but little of me or of his friends in the world. There is that student, Johann Tring—"

"Yes, I know," he answered quickly.

"He and my uncle are together in the loft every

night. Sometimes they stay there until it is light. They say queer things, and sometimes my uncle cries out as if he were in pain. You heard them the night that I told you to go up the staircase. It is always like that."

"I told Father what I heard that night," said Joseph, "and he only said that it was none of our affair, that your uncle is a man who has been very kind to us, and who knows what he is about. Also he forbade me ever to spy upon your uncle again. Father said that your uncle is a great scholar and that he is now probably working upon something that will win him fame."

"Aye—perhaps," she meditated, "but I loved him better as he was."

From that time on Elzbietka became more and more a part of Pan Andrew's family. In the afternoons she used to bring her sewing downstairs into the front room and sit there for hours working and chatting or humming little tunes under her breath. When Joseph returned from his studies in the afternoon the two were accustomed to walk out into the city and see its changing wonders, its new caravans, its pageants, its companies of knights and soldiers, its processions of guilds. Often they walked out through the gates into the country, where there was rich black earth, and behind them or alongside or ahead ran the great Tartar dog. The walks took them to the old Jewish city of the Kazimierz, across the fortified bridge on the west arm of the Vistula, to the old church on the Skalka where the holy Stanislas was murdered at his altar, to the high mound above the city where it was said that old King Krakus was buried; to these and to many other places had they wandered while the sun was bright and the air not too cool.

Once they went to visit the towers of the Church of Our Lady Mary in the late afternoon. The watchman let them in at the little gate at the base of the tower and they climbed up to the room where the day trumpeter was on duty. He was the man that Pan Andrew relieved at night, and he thought it a great honor to have a visit from such a little lady as Elzbietka, and he told her many of the legends which have come down from old days, when the church tower was being built.

Joseph picked up his father's trumpet from the table. "When I first play all the four Heynals you must listen and see if you hear a single note played wrong."

"I will listen."

"If I play a wrong note, I will give you my cap. If I play two, then I will give you Wolf." He smiled then, as a boyish thought came to him. "If I ever play the Heynal through to the end, without stopping at the broken note, then you may run to Jan Kanty and tell him to summon the watch, for then something will have happened to me."

"How do you mean?" She was, as ever, serious, though he was smiling.

"You know the story of this hymn, the Heynal?"

"Yes," she answered.

"How, when the Tartars burned the city, the trumpeter stayed on duty and played the hours as he had sworn?"

"Yes . . . A brave story."

"Well"—Joseph liked to see the blue eyes widen
—"one night the Tartars will attack the city, or
perhaps the Knights of the Cross. I shall see them
coming from afar, in the midst of fire and smoke,
and I shall hear war cries and their horses' hoofs.
And I shall be all alone in the tower that night, for
neither my father nor any person will be here. And
when I realize that it is an enemy, I must have a
signal, since I myself may not leave the tower—a
signal to someone in the town who will give the
alarm. So I will play the Heynal, but I will not stop
on the broken note. That note does not end the
measure, you know. I will play on, two or three
notes further."

"Excellent," she cried, and her cheeks were red
with the excitement of it. "If I hear you play the
Heynal without stopping at the broken note, I will
run straight to Jan Kanty."

"Now come look at the city," he broke off conversation on the subject. He was a little ashamed,
for he had not expected Elzbietka to take his remarks quite so seriously. She had not taken the
trumpet signal as the jest he intended, but had re-
joiced at it, as do most young people when they
have a secret with some important person. And, to
her, Joseph was a person of very great importance,
not only because of his prowess with the trumpet
and his progress in the collegium but because, indeed, he possessed somehow more than ordinary
seriousness for a boy of his age.

They peered through a little window. Off to the
right ran the Street of St. Florian, with the gate and
church beyond: new towers were being constructed

that very year in the walls that ran about the city, and two of them near the Florian Gate were visible from the tower of the Church of Our Lady Mary. To each city guild was assigned one of these towers, to be kept in repair and to be manned in case of attack on the city. The joiners' and the tailors' guilds had watchtowers near this gate. Between these watchtowers and the church were many palaces with large enclosures in the center, open to the sun, where guards and soldiers were working or waiting or disporting themselves, breaking each other's heads with quarterstaves, or fencing, or shooting with arrows at pigeons tied to the tops of high poles.

Directly below them the market was still busy, although it was late afternoon, for the peasants were ready to sell at small profit what remained of their stock and go home; under the arches of the Cloth Hall the crowds were still passing from booth to booth, examining the laces and embroidery and fine silks that had come in from the east and south; beyond the Cloth Hall rose the tower of the Town House, or Ratusz, and in front of it two luckless wretches struggled in the pillory while a crowd of urchins pelted them with mud and decayed vegetables. To the left rose the peak of the Church of the Franciscans—they passed to the south window and there saw the twin towers of the old Church of St. Andrew, and far beyond it the great rock citadel, the Wawel, with its palace and cathedral glorious in the afternoon sun.

There were blue shadows already lengthening across the market when they descended from the tower and crossed the market square. Against the palaces that lined the open space there were more shadows, and moving like shadows within these shadows promenaded black-gowned students and masters. They were moving definitely in one direction, and when once caught up in the crowd, Joseph and Elzbietka followed, unresisting, for they knew that some excitement was afoot in the students' quarter.

The black figures grew constantly more and more numerous, until at length the two stopped and pushed right and left in an endeavor to reach a position of vantage in front of the dormitory in St. Ann's Street. The dormitory was set back from the street, and in front was an open court, grassed over, in the center of which was a stone statue of Kazimir the Great, the founder of the university. Here, upon the pedestal of this statue, leaning back upon the throne which bore Kazimir, stood a man in the gown of a master of arts, speaking to the assembled students in the Latin language.

"I heard of him today," Joseph told Elzbietka. "He is a celebrated Italian scholar who comes here to read the writings of the master poets and to recite some verses of his own. He talks of poets who bear such names as Dante and Petrarch, and he says that the day will come when a new learning will rule the world. He says that men have been in darkness too long, that the barbarism which fell upon the world after the downfall of Rome will be done away with only when men write in their native tongues and think for themselves."

"And can you really understand him when he speaks?"

"After a fashion. He speaks Latin, as do all our masters and priests and scholars. My father had teachers for me when I was eight years old, and since then I have worked much with the Latin tongue. At first it pleased me not at all, for there were rules and tables and grammar, but when I began to understand that Latin would admit me into the proudest society of the world, then I began to like it better. In the months that I have been here my teaching has all been in Latin, and I hope, myself, to be able to speak it fluently sometime. I can understand much, though not all."

"Why does not this Italian poet speak, then, in the university?"

"He might, perhaps—but to a certain extent it would stir up strife, since there are those among the masters who do not like the New Learning, as it is called. Our old teachings are all of the great Aristotle, and yet we have never read anything of him in the Greek language—everything that we study is in Latin. We have many treatises upon learning which the masters have used for centuries, and most of them do not desire to change their ways."

The Italian scholar at that moment began to read his own verses in the Latin tongue. He had scarcely finished, amid much acclaim, when a Polish scholar mounted the pedestal and began to read some of his verses written in the Polish language.

"Why do they not all do that?" asked Elzbietka. "One can understand them so much better. If I were a poet, I should not think of writing in an old language that no one speaks except a few scholars. I would write of Poland and its flowers; I would write of the trumpeter in the tower and the blue sky that one sees behind the castle on Wawel Hill. Truly, I like this New Learning as you call it."

Joseph smiled but knew not what to say.

"And," she continued, "why is not this learning as good for women as it is for men? Why is it that all writings of poets and scholars and men of learning should be read only by men? I would read such writings too."

It was said with such gravity and such an air of wisdom that at first Joseph was inclined to smile, but as he looked into her face and saw the seriousness there, he desisted.

"Truly," he said finally, "I know not why you should not read as do men, but I know of no woman who ever entered the university."

As they turned through a short lane from St. Ann's Street to the Street of the Pigeons they failed to notice a pair of men conversing quietly behind the buttress of a house on the farther side. Both were of short stature, and one was much bent —as he spoke he raised his long, lean fingers close to his mouth:

"Sh-h. . . . That is the boy."

The other started and turned quickly, but appeared puzzled. "When did you say he came?"

The bent-over man, who was no other than Stas, son of the woman who lived in the court, gave the date to a day.

"Then it must be he," exclaimed the other. "On

the day that I saw him he was dressed like a country youth and his clothes were dusty from travel. Today he is arrayed in velvet like any prince and has besides the cap of a junior collegian. But his stature is the same. And you say that he lives above you?"

"Yes. Goes by the name of Kovalski."

"H'm—it was Charnetski when I knew him. . . . Now, you, look at me—do you seě this piece of gold? That's true gold, red gold, an' will buy many a dainty or many a drink. That is to be yours, for your very own."

Stas almost shrieked for joy when the stranger put the piece of money in his hand.

"But, look you—no talking about this anywhere else. This is my business, mine and yours, and I tell you that when we are finished there will be more gold pieces for you just like that. Now show me the place where they live."

They followed along until Joseph and Elzbietka stood before the entrance to the court.

"That is the place," said Stas.

"Well and good. Now keep a close watch and let me know anything that is new. I will be at the Inn of the Golden Elephant every afternoon at the third hour, but do not tell anyone there that you are looking for me. Let your words be only for my ears. And remember, the lantern in the man's face tonight. There will be much gold for you. You understand?"

The man did. His very shoulders seemed to chuckle at the thought of it. He let himself into the court and went at once to his room.

In the meantime the other walked briskly to the inn and sat down at a table. His thoughts were dancing in his head, for by an extraordinary piece of luck he had succeeded in locating the family of Pan Andrew. Luck indeed it was, because never, if he had come upon him face to face in the street, would he have known Joseph at all. It was only because Stas had named him as the son of the man who went abroad only by night that he could see any resemblance to that boy who had sent his horse flying away through the mud on that morning so many weeks before. For this man was that same one who called himself Stefan Ostrovski.

They disappeared that day after the riot—he thought to himself as he sat in the inn—and were nowhere to be found. The earth might have opened and swallowed them whole. No other Charnetski in Krakow answered their description—I had well given them up for lost, and with them, a castle and coffers of gold in the Ukraine. For when Ivan, himself, promises, then there is profit to be had. I return to the Ukraine, but there is no word from them there. My men are even now riding from city to city in the vain hunt. Meanwhile I, answering some tiny voice of wisdom that speaks from somewhere into my ear, come back here.

He struck the table with his fist. "Men call me Bogdan Grozny—Bogdan the Terrible," he exclaimed. "But terror often has brains. This venture has begun in luck and must end well. And once I get what I seek from that white-faced Pole he shall rue the day of my humiliation at the Krakow

Gate." And with the thought of that adventure, a look of hatred came into his eyes.

His attention was diverted for the moment by the sight of a beggar with a dirty bandage across his face working from table to table at the inn, begging for alms in a whining tone.

As the beggar came near, the man dropped a coin in the outstretched hand and whispered, "You come late today."

"Pardon me, master, I thought I had a scent."

The beggar seemed to expect a blow, and assumed a defensive attitude, when the man smiled.

"No matter, the work is done," he whispered. "Mount your horse tonight and ride like the wind for Tarnov. There you will send out our brothers to bring in the men who are hunting. It may take three weeks—but hurry before the first fall of snow comes."

The beggar took the orders, ambled out of the inn quietly, just as he had come in, and proceeded in like fashion until he was well along the street which skirts the market on the west. Then, suddenly stepping behind a house buttress, he tore the bandage from his face and ran with all speed for the gate on the Mogilev Road, in order to get through unchallenged before the night watch came on duty. He passed through, sauntered down the road until he came to a small peasant cottage with a stable in the rear; here he found the horse which he had ridden to Krakow, and with a single word to the owner of the house, who seemed to understand his movements fully, galloped off to the distant bridge where ran the Tarnov Road.

The man at the inn continued to ruminate. That stoop-shouldered misbegotten thing that calls himself Stas came to us like an angel from heaven. Often had I noticed him in here, talking and making free with all the beggars, and even at first look of him, I thought to myself that here was such a man as might serve a purpose for me sometime. So I have the landlord bring him a friendly glass, and talking as he drinks it, he drops a word about the new trumpeter who never goes forth in the daytime!

That is the boy as sure as man can be sure, despite his new trappings of velvet; and then the fact that there are three of them, and the date of their arrival. Tonight when the trumpeter leaves by the door, Stas will hold the lantern to his face, and I, hiding near by, will see—but there is scarce need of that, it is as well as proved. My men will be here in a week or two, and it will be but short work after that.

His face was working pale in his excitement—it was all white save the button mark which stood out on it like a clot of blood.

What would the honorable Pan Andrew have said that day—he chuckled—had he known that Bogdan Grozny was before him? For he, and every man in the Ukraine, knows Peter of the Button Face. That was a good name I gave him—Ostrovski! Ostrovski of the proud family of Chelm that once called me slave.

Peter of the Button Face was indeed a name feared everywhere in the Ukraine. It had been bestowed upon this man, whose real name was Bogdan, chiefly by the Poles, for among the Cossacks he was known as Grozny, or Terrible. A savage outcast, born of a Tartar mother and Cossack father, he had been involved in every dark plot on the border in the last ten years. Houses he had burned by the score, and men and women he had put to death cruelly. Under his command was a band of ruffians who would rise up suddenly in the Ukraine, overnight almost, and set out upon any adventure of fire and sword that he suggested.

He was not despised by great folk either—Polish or Muscovite—when there was unlawful work to be done; nobles often employed him for unscrupulous tasks that they dared not perform themselves; the Great Khan of the Tartars even had dispatched him on a mission among the Golden Horde; his name was a power on both sides of the boundary, for in Poland also he had confederates who served him.

And at the present time the great country of the Ukraine, which had come to Poland through the marriage of Jagiello of Lithuania with Jadviga of Poland about one hundred years previous—this huge land was full of plots and counterplots in the struggle for mastery between Muscovy and Poland. Ivan of Moscow had already begun to turn envious eyes upon this territory, which had been the heart of the old Byzantine Russia with Kiev as its capital, and was making plans to wrest it from Poland at the first opportunity. And in such fashion many a dweller such as Pan Andrew Charnetski found himself bereft of property and fields in a single night. For there were many such as Bogdan the

Terrible, or as the Poles knew him, Peter of the Button Face, who were ready at a minute's notice to engage in some such fearful task with rewards of plunder and captives for their work.

However, little realizing what savage forces had been let loose against them, the family of Pan Andrew sat down to a quiet supper.

9

Button-Face Peter Attacks

Cold weather came in late November—or Listopad, the month of Falling Leaves, as Polish folk call it—and found the poor people in the villages already fortified in their log huts with the thatched roofs. Sand had been heaped high about the walls of the houses, all crevices that led to the outer world were stopped up with mud or tree branch or stone, wood and charcoal were piled under table and bench, and from the ceiling hung dried vegetables and mushrooms and sausage. The geese and pigs still ran about outside the house but would be taken in with the first frost, to share the "black" or large compartment of the hut with the family. In the second or "white" compartment of the hut the whole family slept when the weather was not too frigid, but when the snow was up to the roof level, and the cold was so great that one could hear trees cracking in the night, all slept in the "black" room which had not even a chimney to vent the smoke that poured out steadily from an open fireplace.

In the city houses, wealthy men were beginning

to build high tile stoves of Italian pattern, but for the most part, people depended for heat and comfort upon the open fireplace. When the first frost came boys ran hither and thither with flaming coals for starting the first fires; up in the tower of the Church of Our Lady Mary the watchmen kept eyes constantly wide open to detect as quickly as possible the patches of flame which sometimes broke out from the roofs of overheated dwellings, and many a troublesome night was spent by the water master and his men quenching such fires.

A light snow was falling on the last Wednesday of the month, when Pan Andrew started for his nightly duties at the church. The world had been going well with him, he reflected, as he made his way through the dark and well-nigh deserted streets: his son was making marked progress in the collegium, his wife was happy and contented, he himself was earning enough to support them both comfortably, and he hoped that before long he would have a chance to present his offering to the king. For it had not been possible thus far to gain an audience; either the king had been away on business in Torun with soldiers and diplomats, or he was in Vilna, the home of the Jagiello dynasty, which now ruled Poland, or in Lvov, where the Ruthenian subjects lived.

In the short snatches of time when he had been in Krakow neither Pan Andrew nor Jan Kanty had been able to reach him, because so many had been waiting ahead of them—the ambassadors from the Czechs who came to offer him the crown of Bohemia, the delegation from Rome, the scholars from Italy, the deputation from the Teutonic Knights asking for a compact against the Hussites, and other men of title and power.

This delay was no great cause of concern to Pan Andrew, however, since an audience was eventually assured. Late in the summer Jan Kanty had sent a petition to the very throne itself, and the king had advised the gentle scholar by message that he would see him at the first opportunity. In the meanwhile the treasure seemed hidden in as safe quarters as Pan Andrew could ask for.

It was several hours after Pan Andrew had left his lodgings on the Street of the Pigeons that there came a violent ringing of the bell that summoned Stas. Stas unfastened the door and thrust his lantern directly into the face of the man who stood there, and for his pains was rewarded with a smart blow upon the chin which tumbled him into the soft snow which was now beginning to cover everything.

"Don't do that again as you value your life," the stranger muttered as he picked up the fallen lantern and straightened the limp Stas upon his feet. "You fool, don't you know that someone might have seen my face? If some watchman took me, he would as well take you; it is for your safety that no man knows anything of this meeting. Is everything ready?"

"Yes," responded Stas a bit ruefully.

"Then tell me, who is in the building?"

"Well—there is the lodger on the top floor and his niece, and there is the boy and his mother."

"The students?"

"They have gone to a discussion at the Hungarian pension. Sometimes they do not return before daybreak."

"Good! Then we can work without fear. A dozen men will suffice, four to enter the rooms of Pan Andrew, four to quiet the tenants if need be, and four to stand at the gate. If the guard should come, we can silence him."

"Will you see the stairs?"

"Yes, they live—"

"Up one flight." They ascended the stairs, Stas in the lead. It seemed to the stranger that the staircase swayed a little beneath their feet.

"We must take care here," he muttered. "It seems as if a weight would bring this down."

Just then a dog began to bark in the court below.

"What is that?" demanded the man, turning on Stas. "You did not tell me of a dog."

"He is chained," replied the other. "Will you give me the gold now?"

"Here." The man thrust him a few coins. He took them greedily and felt them over in the darkness, for the stranger was holding under his coat the lantern that he had picked up from the ground.

"This is not all?" Stas' voice rose to a whine.

"Swine!" For a moment the man lost control of himself. "Here is the rest, then," and he swung his free hand to Stas' throat, and sank his fingers in the flesh. Stas fought but could not release himself from those fingers that dug like iron points—at length the man freed him.

"No more of that," he admonished. "The next time you will find yourself in paradise, or some other world. Listen, fool, once and for all—if all goes well here, I will give you double of that which you already have. But if you betray me, or make one foolish blunder, then you will receive, not gold, but a punishment that is worse than anything you dream of."

Stas beat a retreat down the stairs, the stranger behind him.

"Remember," was the final admonishment, "we will be here just after the second hour has sounded. Let us in, and your part in this is finished."

Now it so happened than Pan Kreutz, the alchemist, was working alone in the loft above his room that night. He had already finished one experiment, and was about to begin a more difficult one, when his attention was caught by the sudden barking of a dog in the court beneath.

What can that be? he thought. There is no moon to cause barking, nor does the dog bark at any of the dwellers in the court.

He quickly threw a covering over the lantern that lighted the loft, and opened the door so that he might look down.

His suspicions that all was not well in the court were confirmed in the next second, when he heard a whispered conversation somewhere below, while the stairs creaked as if two persons were ascending. Then all at once came an exclamation of pain in a voice that he recognized as Stas'.

More whispering, and the footsteps descended.

The next instant the alchemist, leaning forward to listen, heard the stranger's final instruction to Stas.

There is, then, some mischief afoot, he decided. Doorkeepers do not let honest visitors into any house at two o'clock in the morning.

He re-entered the attic room, and uncovered the lantern after making fast the door. For some time he puzzled about what he had heard. Who was the stranger, and what business did he have with Stas, the watchman? And what ought he to do about it? He was for a moment minded to notify the night watch.

I am perhaps magnifying things, he finally concluded. More than likely two o'clock on the morrow was meant. Besides, I myself could give any marauder here a very warm reception—he glanced about the loft. The thought seemed to please him, for he chuckled for the space of a moment, and then turned seriously to his work.

For an hour or more his experiment, which was difficult and exacting, held all his attention. But when it was finally finished and the results carefully noted, the thought of Stas and his mysterious visitor returned to him. In the stillness of the late hour the affair seemed to show a graver face.

He jumped up suddenly and set the fires leaping in two braziers. He melted a gum in one of them and heated some liquid in the other. At length at the end of fifteen minutes he covered the fires and took out the substances. With a small brush he smeared the mixture of the two over his long student gown that hung against the wall. Then he took the mask which he used when making experiments with certain poisonous gases, and covered this with the same drug he had compounded in the braziers —the gum causing it to cling to the surface of the mask.

I have but to sprinkle this with aqua phosphorata, he said to himself, and the heavens will not be more brilliant than I.

He sat back in his chair to wait, and with closed eyes tried to reason it all out. What can be the meaning of this? he thought. The stranger with Stas stopped on the landing of Pan Andrew's lodging. What mystery can have attached itself to this family? Why should the name be changed? Who would seek revenge upon a man and a woman and a boy? Elzbietka has found a mother, and I good friends. They have no treasure with them, no money of any kind, for even on that first day Pan Andrew was obliged to sell his cart and horses for the means of living.

He was becoming drowsy, for he had worked much of late, and had had but little sleep, and he was on the point of succumbing to his weariness when he heard the watchman at the Church of Our Lady Mary strike twice upon the bell and then begin to play the Heynal. The fourth Heynal was scarcely finished when he heard a motion in the court below. It was Stas creeping along the wall in order to open the door. Throwing back his door noiselessly the alchemist lay flat on the floor and leaned out over the threshold. The door below creaked a little as it opened. Someone came in. The alchemist listened: One—two—three—more!

By the lightning, there must be a dozen of them, if footsteps tell no lies. I did wrong not to notify the watch. If I shout now, he may come, but there are enough to silence both him and me. No, I have made my beer and I must drink it.

Next the stairs began to creak, and almost instantly the hoarse barking of a dog cut through the air.

"Silence that dog," he heard someone whisper from the steps. Footsteps were heard again in the court as if someone had gone back to combat the animal. At this same moment the door leading into the court was slammed shut, and there was a rattle of the chain that fastened it on the inside.

A precious jewel, that Stas, thought the alchemist. He shall pay for this tomorrow.

A cry of pain rang out suddenly from below. It was the cry not of a dog, but of a man. Ha, thought Pan Kreutz, Wolf finished that one.

There was a sound of a man running across the court. "I can't get near him without injury," he whispered loudly to the leader of the party. "He sank his teeth in my leg, and I am faint for pain."

"Three of you attack him at once," directed the leader.

There was scuffling again, and suddenly the night was made hideous with the mad howling and barking of Wolf and the shrieking of men in pain; at this moment Joseph, with a light in his hand, appeared at the door on the second story:

"Wolf—Wolf," he called.

He did not call again.

Whew, thought the alchemist, they silenced the boy. A gag, probably.

He was right. The leader of the attacking party had seized Joseph and thrown a cloth bag over his head.

"To the house," he shouted to the men below. "Four of you stand guard at the door. Four of you wait at the stairs and let no one descend, and the rest come with me."

As the light of the lantern which he had taken from the boy swung upon his face, the man watching above could see that it was marked with a great round scar like an immense button.

"Tartar or Cossack," he exclaimed, "for the plague which leaves such scars is an Eastern plague; these men have come from a long distance."

He was right. This was indeed the band of that ruffian whom the Poles called Peter of the Button Face and whose bad fame men knew in all the Ukraine and the lands to the east.

In the next second, almost, they were inside the house—Peter, and three men following. There came to the alchemist's ears the scream of a woman, followed by a crash as if she had been thrown upon the floor. Then came the sound of the breaking of furniture, of the tearing up of matting, of the destruction of everything within the house as if a quick, violent search was being made. The door was open and the alchemist could hear clearly all the sounds below.

"Look in the bed," the leader spoke.

Pan Andrew and his wife slept in a large bed in the front room. Swords were quickly at work ripping this to pieces. They cut open the pillows, they tore apart the blankets, and it was only after the bed was a complete ruin that the leader found what he had been seeking.

"There it is," he shouted; "that large package, done up in cloth."

With his sword he ripped away the layers of cloth that bound it—one by one they fell upon the floor until the object he sought stood uncovered in his right hand. But just at that instant, as he was about to dart for the door, there came a shrill voice, shrieking, "My gold—my gold!"

Peter turned like a flash. "Blood of a dog—"

The lantern was held up. Its light disclosed the face of Stas, maddened with fear that he should not receive the price of his treachery.

"Gold! I'll give you gold," shouted Peter, infuriated. "Someone take him and throw him down to the dog. Then he can take what gold we choose to throw him."

Two men seized him, but he fought madly and dashed into the room. There the third man headed him off and the two others fell upon him from behind; his slim body wriggled loose, however, and he fell across the table already overturned by the intruders in their search for Pan Andrew's treasure and clung there with ferociousness to the upturned legs. He kicked, he bit, he struck out blindly—but they tore him loose just as Peter set the prize on the floor to take the man in hand himself.

The lantern rested on the floor behind him, and as the struggling men swung toward him, Stas, shot with a brilliant idea, worked a leg loose and kicked the lantern over. As it fell, the door swung open and the candle went out. Almost instantly, however, the ruffians closed their grip upon him and hustled him to the door.

Over the rail he would have gone without further ceremony had not there come the sudden screaming of a girl from the floor above.

"The plague upon them all," exclaimed Peter, dropping Stas. "Here everything is as smooth as water in a lake, then all of a sudden babies and fools raise the dead with their cries. Come, we have enough—let us get out of this at once."

He groped his way back to Pan Andrew's bed, and was feeling in the dark for the precious thing that was the object of his raid, when there came a crash like that of thunder from above, and through the open door appeared a terrible red light that seemed to come from the sky and enveloped everything for the moment in a garment of red.

10

The Evil One Takes a Hand

Peter rushed to the door and stood, staring.

Balls of red fire were shooting out into the air from the opened casement of the room in the loft, flooding the place with light as they burst with terrific explosions. In the light Peter could see his men standing horror-struck, four below him at the bottom of the stairs, and four on guard at the door. Those who had been clinging to Stas on the landing had recoiled in fright before the fiery balls, and the half-wit had seized the opportunity to slink stealthily away through their legs, and make for the lower steps.

For a moment Peter stood motionless. In bodily things he was braver than the brave, but in the face of such magic as this he was a coward; yet though he trembled, he realized that he must play a man's part if he wished to keep the leadership of his band, and accordingly, spurring himself up to a pitch of bravado, he rushed up the stairs from the second floor to the third and stood there just as another bomb soared out into the air.

"Come back! Come back!" they were shouting from below.

"Come up! Come up!" he commanded. "What are you frightened of?"

"It is the Evil One himself!"

Peter shook his curved Cossack sword in the darkness. "Come up—come up, I tell you, you cowardly dogs—come up or I'll separate your coward heads from your useless bodies. Come up, I say—come up!"

And so much was he feared, that the three men on the second-floor crossed themselves in the manner of the Greek Church and went creeping up after him.

"We have the treasure," pleaded the nearest man in a trembling voice, "let us escape from here. This is nothing human. This is the work of the Evil One. Devils are abroad and a man is not sure of his soul."

"Devils," roared Peter, "bones and fiddlesticks! Come up here, you, and be men. This is no devil. This some joker who values his head but lightly. If we do not silence him, he will alarm the whole city before we get back to the gate."

"Up that," he commanded a second later, shoving the first man against the staircase to the loft. "Up that, and tell us what you see."

The man mounted, trembling violently, for he was sure that the powers of darkness themselves were working against them.

"The door is open here," he whispered, "and no lights within." A man below him on the stairway passed the word along to Peter.

"Then up, every mother's son of you," ordered the leader. "There is a man there. Put a knife in his throat and descend quickly."

The rest pulled themselves up and entered the loft. After a few minutes of impatient waiting Peter climbed the steps himself and pushed himself across the dark threshold.

"What have you found?" he demanded impatiently.

"Nothing," the answer came faintly from one corner of the loft.

"If there is anyone here let him speak now," Peter bellowed. His voice drowned the quiet opening of the door of a closet in the back of the room. "If we find anyone, it will go hard—"

Like a bolt of lightning out of a clear sky the loft was suddenly illuminated with a glow of red fire as there leaped into existence out of the blackness of the night the very incarnation of the Evil One in his worst mood. Clad in fiery garments which smelled of fire and brimstone and which seemed to blaze and burn and give off a greenish smoke and flame, he moved slowly forward, waving in his right hand a scepter of flaming red which was crackling with heat as a green bough crackles when it burns, while from its end little balls of fire were dripping.

It was so sudden, so unexpected, this apparition in a pitchblack world of night, of a red, fiery, glowing devil, that Peter, stouthearted as he was, let out a sudden shriek, and trembled like a leaf.

But if he trembled, the others went mad with

fear. "Out! Out!" they shrieked, crowding to the stairway.

Upon their heels came the fantastic demon waving his scepter right and left and favoring first one and then another with smart blows, as they fought to be first at the stairway. Two reached it at one time and went scrambling down, to be joined by the third a second later, who came tumbling down upon them just as they gained the third-floor landing.

Peter, however, stood his ground for a moment. Turning about at the head of the stairs he shouted, "Be you man or demon, I will see what you have in you," and rushed with his drawn sword upon the weird figure. That one simply stood aside as he rushed, and waved his hand in the direction of the man's face.

"Ahew—ahew!" the brigand screamed with pain, for something choking and powdery was filling his eyes and throat. "Help—cowards—I am in the hands of a thousand devils. Help, I say!"

There was no sound outside save the noise of the men scrambling down the next stairway.

Peter stumbled blindly to the steps and fairly slid down them, fearful lest the phantom should follow and give him another dose. But the phantom, though following, did not repeat his attack; he came slowly down the stairs after the retreating party, hurling little bombs of colored fire into the air, which as they exploded flooded the court with lights of rainbow hues.

Below, the din was deafening. The dog had worked his head loose from the bag which had been thrown over it, and was barking at the top of his lungs. Men were shouting and crying out in terror, forgetful of caution and the necessity for silence. Joseph, who had been gagged and bound in the rear room of the family's dwelling, had gotten his feet loose from the ropes and was kicking with all his force against the wooden partition wall, Elzbietka was crying out for aid, and heads were beginning to emerge from open casements in all the adjoining buildings. Someone in the street outside was calling loudly for the watch, and Stas, having rescued himself from one predicament, was for no reason at all pulling at the rope of the bell that hung over the door, its clamor adding to the general uproar.

On the landing at the second floor the three retreating ruffians collided with the four men standing there and almost toppled them into the court. They had barely regained their balance when the lower supports of the stairs, which had been groaning already from the unaccustomed weight and traffic, suddenly collapsed and catapulted the whole company, amidst indescribable turmoil, into the court below. Peter, coming behind the three, managed to save himself by leaping nimbly to the threshold of Pan Andrew's dwelling, but the flaming figure behind him remained momentarily on the stairs above the second floor where the supports and staircase held firm. Not for long did he remain there, however, for as Peter turned his back to disappear into the house, the pursuer leaped from the lower step of the remaining stairway and landed squarely upon Peter, hurling him with a crash to the floor well inside the front room of Pan Andrew's dwelling.

Below in the court there was a veritable pandemonium: the crashing apart of beam and beam where the staircase struck the ground, the shrieking of the frightened, the moaning of the injured—for two men had been pinned beneath the fallen staircase—the terror and distraction of the ruffians on guard below, whose one idea now was to escape through the outer door before the arrival of the watch.

While all this was transpiring in the court, the alchemist, who with his chemicals and powders had caused all the trouble, shook his heavy scepter, a club smeared with glowing resin, in the face of Peter, who lay prostrate beneath him, and demanded:

"Now—what do you seek here?"

But Peter had gotten some of his courage back, and besides the voice sounded more like that of a man than a devil. "I will not tell!"

"You will!"

"I will not."

"You will be turned over to the watch."

"I care not. They can learn nothing."

"First let us have another look at you."

He carefully drew a fireball from a fold of his gown, keeping his weight upon the man under him and holding one hand at his throat. The ball he ignited by rubbing it against the floor, and when it was burning he tossed it upon the stone hearth. There was a flash of light and the room was suddenly as bright as even day could make it.

But, after all, he did not look at Peter! For there was something else in the room that claimed his attention at once. It was the large round object that Peter had sought in Pan Andrew's bed—there it lay upon the floor a short arm's length away, gleaming like a thousand prisms of finest glass.

"Oho," he exclaimed, "oho! So that's it. Well, Pan Robber, it seems that your expedition was no ordinary one. No common house looting, this. . . . Lie still there, or I'll sink these fingers into your windpipe," for Peter had tried to wriggle to one side while the alchemist's attention was taken with the new object.

"Who sent you here?" demanded the latter.

Peter was silent.

"But you must talk. Do you hear that—below?"

It was the night watch shouting, "Stand, in the name of the king."

Peter, whose courage was now revived, since he realized that it was a man and not a devil that he was dealing with, decided to try a little strategy.

"I will tell you all if you will hide me here."

"I give no promises. But tell me what you know."

"Then see that." He twisted one hand away from his captor as if to point toward the shining object on the floor, which was now gleaming like a miniature sun in the last rays of the nearly burned-out fireball.

"I see it." The alchemist glanced at it; the instant's relaxation proved fatal, however, for with the moment, the under man's right hand came clear and tore the alchemist's grip from his throat.

In the struggle that followed, the alchemist was no match for the lithe and wiry Cossack. They rolled back and forth across the floor, tight in each other's arms, they broke table legs, they brought down crockery from the shelves, they crashed into walls—and through all this the Cossack little by little overcame the advantage which the other had held in the beginning. First he twisted his legs in such fashion that he caught Pan Kreutz's body as if in a vise, a trick that he had learned in the old days in the Ukraine; then he snapped his hands free from the other's grip and wound his arms in under his shoulders. Tighter and tighter he drew arms and legs, until the alchemist's bones began to send out cracking noises; then, with a quick movement, he had reversed their positions and it was he who was on top and the alchemist underneath. Smash! He had bumped the man's head against the floor with all his force, a blow sufficient to stun a giant, and in an instant had tossed him against the wall.

There the alchemist lay.

Like a panther moving to attack, Peter seized the object which he had come to procure, and leaped for the door.

He did not reach it unscathed. Pan Kreutz had also a last stratagem. It was fortunate for him that when the Cossack bumped his head against the floor, it was his mask that had borne the brunt of the blow—otherwise it is doubtful if he could ever have risen. But when the Cossack tossed him aside he lay there feigning unconsciousness, and as the other turned, he reached with a swiftness as quick as Peter's into a pocket of his gown, where he had concealed a small package of explosive powder which might be ignited only by concussion. A wonder it was indeed that the powder had not exploded while they were wrestling on the floor.

This Pan Kreutz poised in his right hand as Peter made for the door. In another second the man would be gone—the alchemist caught his balance and hurled the package with all his strength.

It was a fair shot! It caught the Cossack with full force square on the back of the head and burst with a loud report.

Those below, now already turning their attention to the noise and the confusion on the second floor, heard the sharp explosion and saw the court flooded with light. In the midst of the glare there came a shriek that seemed to stir every corner of the courtyard, and almost immediately a man with hair flaming and garments streaked with fire sprang from the threshold of Pan Andrew's lodging to the edge of the stairway that had not collapsed, and darted to the floor above. He stopped there only for one fleeting glance below. The court, blazing with torches and alive with tumult, was full of figures—students, watchmen, soldiers—so that escape that way was impossible. He leaped to the loft stairway and mounted it. Clutching at the roof, which was not far above his head, he swung the low door back until it lay alongside the house and then climbed over it to the roofing. Along this he rushed like a meteor, his blazing hair streaming behind him in a trail of sparks—he leaped to an adjoining roof, and then to another, until he came to a place where the roofs sloped down to a wall, and there he was seen last.

A hue and cry was set up, but the man had escaped. Some said that he ran along the top of the wall and leaped into a monastery garden beyond— others that he only pretended to descend and had crept back among the housetops. At any rate, he was not discovered.

When temporary stairs were finally put in place the watchmen released Joseph and his mother from the small room in their own quarters where they had lain bound, and brought Elzbietka down to them. Pan Kreutz, who had retired to his loft, where he shed his torn gown and his mask, was bleeding and weak from his struggle and lost no time in getting into his bed. It was thought by all that the robbers had carried away nothing, but when Pan Andrew returned in the morning the house was searched thoroughly, only to find that the treasure was missing. Spectators swore that Peter could not have carried anything with him when he made his perilous escape over the roofs, and a few said that they had noticed that his hands were empty.

However, hunt high or low as they did, the treasure was gone, and Pan Andrew, in spite of the views of the spectators, was fully convinced that the robber had stolen it.

Those of Peter's band who had been injured in the fall of the stairs or had been unable to escape from the court were taken to jail and sentenced to various punishments. Several were put away into dungeons, where they could do no more harm, two were banished "for a period of ninety-nine years," and the rest were delivered to justice in other towns, where they had committed previous crimes. But the most vigorous questioning could get no information from them, and it was concluded that they knew little of the designs of the leader upon Pan Andrew. As for Stas, his mother would have naught of him after this act of treachery. She lost little time in turning him out of her house, and never would she receive him back again. It was heard some time later that he had become a waiter in the Inn of the Golden Elephant, but after the robbery of a guest there one night, he disappeared and was never heard of in Krakow again.

Pan Kreutz, although somewhat unnerved by his share in the encounter, met Pan Andrew in his lodging the next morning and described as fully as he could the man who had been leader in the events of the preceding night. He had scarcely finished when Pan Andrew sprang to his feet and struck the back of his chair with his fist.

"It is as I thought," he exclaimed fiercely, "the man who has assailed me twice before. And now I know for a certainty that it is that half Mongol, half Cossack that calls himself Bogdan and is known as the Terrible throughout the Cossack lands. I have heard of his evil deeds many times, as has every dweller in the Ukraine. And it would be like him indeed to lead this villainy against me. He is a very devil, a man without pity, though I will say a man of the boldest breed that God ever benefited with the gift of breath. We, the Poles of the

Ukraine, knew him as Peter of the Button Face, because of the scar which you have seen upon his right cheek, and by that scar I would doubtless have recognized him on the morning when he attacked me outside the Krakow Gate, had I not believed that he carried on his lawless deeds always nearer the border."

Thus saying, he went sorrowfully to his work of repairing the damage done by the Cossack band.

11

The Attack on the Church

Down in the Ukraine that winter, when men went about from habitation to habitation on the little horses that had noses so pointed that they could poke them through the snow and eat the dry grass of the steppe beneath, it was known that a great change had come over a certain Bogdan, called the Terrible along the Dnieper and Volga, and Peter of the Button Face among the Polish colonists. It was not that he had lost so much hair that certain ones called him behind his back Bogdan of the Singed Locks, that made him sad and contemplative instead of boisterous and ready as he had once been —it was the effect of some failure that brought on despondency and kept him a recluse for several months. When he did return at length to men's sight and began to appear in the taverns, his hair had grown to its accustomed length, and a huge scar that fire had made was nearly healed over. It was hinted, too, that he had made a journey clear up to the land of the Muscovites and had had conference with Ivan, called the Great, but this he did not speak about, and men dared not question him.

Spring came with the month of March in the
year 1462, with peace over all the Dnieper lands,
save where here and there tribes were on the
march, or the Tartars were threatening raids. With
spring, set out Bogdan the Terrible, and with him
traveled as fine a crowd of cutthroats and cattle
stealers as ever the Ukraine knew. They rode to
Rovno, the town of the Level Plain, and then
struck out for Chelm on the border just beyond the
River Bug. They established headquarters in the
Lublin Woods for a time, for the purpose of pillaging, and then hearing that soldiers had been sent
after them, they vanished into the swamplands to
the north and were not heard of again in those
parts.

It seems that Peter had opposed this pillaging
from the first, because he had other work in hand,
but they were tribesmen and wild, fond of robbery
and theft and eager for gain.

At Tarnov, having them well in hand again, he
organized them into a caravan of Armenian rug
merchants and marched them—carts, horses, and
merchants—to Krakow, the great market of the
eastern part of Europe. In Krakow they camped
with their wares in the square on the east side of
the Cloth Hall.

Now the saddest man in Krakow at this time
was Pan Andrew Charnetski—sad because he had
lost, through no fault of his own, a treasure which
he had intended to present to the king of Poland,
and evidently a treasure of great worth since certain men seemed to envy him its possession. Jan

Kanty sought to comfort him, and his wife and son and Elzbietka did much to divert his thoughts from the seriousness of the loss, but on the long nights when he was alone in the tower, moods of depression would often engulf him.

Joseph, knowing this, took to visiting him in the night vigils when it was possible, before holy days and vacations when there was no collegium on the following morning; often he would come with his father at the tenth hour of the night and remain until morning. Sometimes he would take the duties of the watchman while his father slept and sound the Heynals at each hour and inspect the city regularly from each of the tower windows in order to sound the alarm whenever a red tongue of flame leaped into the sky. Joseph had progressed each day in playing the trumpet and could now sound the Heynal as well as his father.

He was in the tower with Pan Andrew on this same night that Peter and his caravan of merchants were encamped in their carts in the market place below the church. The moon was at its full and the shadows of the church towers fell far across the street and market. Down in front of the church doors a watchman with lantern and halberd paced to and fro calling out, as was his custom, the hours as they were sounded from the tower.

He had already called out the first hour when Peter of the Button Face, watching from a cart across the square, decided to make his first move.

"Michael," he called in a loud whisper, "Michael." And at that, a man in a suit of leather with hat to match and thick sandals slid out of the next cart. He had already divested himself of the round turban and blankets that he wore as an Armenian merchant, and his body seemed to move in a constant succession of quiverings and glidings—in fact, he had always been known in the Ukraine as the Snake—and he stood for a moment by his chief's wagon to receive a whispered command in one ear.

Then, true to his name, he wriggled beneath a dozen carts and past the flank of an outhouse near the church to take refuge behind a tree that grew at this corner of the Rynek. Doubled up here, he waited until the watchman should pass in front of the church. He had not long to wait.

Out from the shadows at the base of the church emerged suddenly a man carrying a lantern that threw a star-shaped light about it. This man tested the door to the stairs leading to the trumpeter's tower, found it securely locked, yawned, and struck the paving stones several times in front of the door with his long halberd, as if he were weary of doing nothing. The Snake's eyes sized up this man as his opponent. He was a man perhaps past middle age, clad in a garment of leather over which was a very light chain armor, poorly woven; this fell like a skirt with pointed edges just below the knees. Above the waist the links of armor were a bit heavier, extending over the shoulders and back into long sleeves clear to the wrist, and up past the neck to a kind of head-covering like a cowl, over which he wore a pointed helmet of rough metal. Outside the armor he wore a very short leather vest caught with a belt from which hung a short sword, and across the shoulders just below the neck another belt with a buckle at the left, where the halberd could be secured and balanced.

He passed from the front of the church to the south side, looked about carefully to see if there were any signs of life in the street or square, and finding none, turned away from the church and entered the churchyard at the south, where the moonlight fell brightly upon the old gravestones. Squatting down behind one of these and crossing himself as if in excuse to the people buried there for disturbing their slumbers, he laid his halberd on the ground at his right side and the lantern at the left. Then, reaching into a wallet which he wore at his girdle, he took out a crust of bread and a huge portion of meat. These he began to eat with no suspicion of any interruption.

In this conduct he was justified, for he had been doing this same thing over and over again for many years; there had been no serious duties about the church save perhaps on a holy day when youth on mischief bound would play some trick upon the watchman, and them he could easily dispatch about their business. Thieves seldom troubled churches in this period, and the cemetery itself was guard enough against marauders in a period full of superstition. Up above him the trumpeter kept a much stricter vigil, and all about the town, the watch tried house doors and questioned late passers-by.

"Oh-ho-hum!" he yawned. Such a quiet thing was life!

But—flattened against the church wall behind

him was one whose intention might have disturbed those weary thoughts had the watchman been able to discern it. The Snake had sized up this situation with rapidity and had taken advantage of the moment that the watchman turned his back upon the square to dart into the projecting shadow of a buttress. Edging along the wall, he moved cautiously until he was but a few yards from the tombstone by which the watchman sat.

Plof! The Snake had pounced like a hawk on a mouse.

There was not even a scuffle, so prepared was the intruder and so taken by surprise was the victim. Down went the watchman on his back by the side of the grave, and in a second the deft Michael had bound his scarf tightly about the man's mouth, so that he could not utter a sound. It was the work of a moment as well, to secure the hands and feet with short bits of rope that he carried in his jacket —he was at first minded to cut the man's throat with his own sword, but he feared lest he might make one last dying cry and upset all their plans.

Inside the victim's leather vest he found a huge brass key. This he cut loose from the short chain which held it, and thrust it into his own belt.

Then, making sure that the bonds were secure, he leaped back into the shadow of the church and stole back to the wagon of his chief as deftly as he had come.

"I have bound and gagged the watchman behind yon gravestone," he reported, "and here is the key to the tower door."

A whispered command traveled along the line of

carts. Then there was a general doffing of blankets and turbans, and the band of Peter, in leather jackets and hats, high hose and tall soft boots, stood ready behind their carts to follow the leader into his excellently planned enterprise.

It was but a short distance from the carts to the tower, and Peter led the way, keeping close to the ground in the shadow cast by the tower. They stood at length, about twenty of them, within the shelter of the angle which the tower made with the church.

"Keep close behind me," said the leader, "when we mount the steps, and watch lest there be loose boards in the stairs beneath your feet. The boy is here this night in the tower with his father. Mount carefully, but rush and secure both father and son when I give you word."

Here he fitted the key, which Michael had stolen from the watchman, to the lock and swung the small iron door on its hinges. He had to stoop as he went in.

"Quiet," he whispered, "follow closely."

In a very few minutes they were all inside. The last man, following directions, closed the iron door, so that if a curious passer-by should inspect it, he would find it shut as it was usually.

"The task is easy," whispered Peter when they had climbed the narrow steps that led to the stairs built in the tower scaffolding. "We have now but to bag our rabbit. But you must see to it that he is not a noisy rabbit. If he once gets his hand on a bell rope, he will awaken the whole town with his ringing. He must be secured quickly."

They went up and up, mounting quietly the stairs that wound about the heavy scaffolding, and treading ever carefully so that not a single board should squeak. At last the leader stopped.

"The light is just ahead," he whispered.

Through the opened door of the tower room came suddenly the voice of Joseph, "You can sleep for the rest of the night, Father," he said. "I will sound the Heynal at every hour; the hourglass is plain to read, and I shall make no error."

It was lucky to hit upon a night when they were together, thought Peter. We can bind the old one and make the young one show us the way to the prize.

Joseph had just spread a manuscript before him on the table in the tower room and had moved a taper close to it to begin reading, when he heard a sudden noise just outside the door. Turning about sharply, he was just in time to see the door thrown violently open, and then three men rushed toward him before he could even assume a defensive attitude; he was absolutely powerless. One man held his arms as closely gripped as in a vise while the two others leaped upon Pan Andrew as he rose, dazed with astonishment, from the little bed.

A fourth man stood in the doorway. His hands were at his hips and he laughed merrily. "Ho—ho—my merry singing birds," he said. "We meet again high up above the noisy world, where none can come to disturb us." Then his brows darkened and he asked, "Do you know why I am here?"

Joseph shuddered. This man was the same that

had met his father on the first day that he had seen
Krakow—this was the man that had incited the
crowd in the Rynek to stone his people—this was
the voice that he had heard while he lay bound
hand and foot in the small room of his lodgings.
But at the same time he wondered what had
brought the man back to the city. He had already
obtained the prize, Joseph thought, after the risk
and danger of the first trial. Was it, perhaps, that
he wished to avenge himself upon his father for
the incident of the cart?

Joseph made a motion as if to cross himself at
thought of this, for here they were high up in the
air above the city, and nothing would be easier
than to hurl a man from the summit into the graveyard below, and none would know of it until morning came and they found the lifeless victim.

Pan Andrew, however, looked at the intruder
steadily. "No," he said, very deliberately, "I do not
know why you are here. But I do know you now,
Peter of the Button Face, sometimes called Bogdan—it is strange that I did not recognize you that
morning when you threatened me."

Peter took notice in no way of Pan Andrew's
latter statement. He heard only the negative answer. Apparently he had not expected it.

"You do not? You lie! . . . Do you think that I
do not know everything?" He pushed his way in
and held the candle close to the prisoner's face. "I
say to you that I have come all this way to get
what I want; I have the means for doing it, too,
and I have men in this company that would rather

see a dog like you dead than alive. Now come—if you value your skin. Where have you hidden the Great Tarnov Crystal?"

Joseph leaped with a thrill. This, then, was the prize that they had brought from the Ukraine—a crystal, the "Great Tarnov Crystal," whose loss the father had not ceased to mourn. But, after all, was a crystal something that men valued so highly? If it were a diamond or a precious stone, there might be some reason for so much covetousness, but a mere crystal—why, he himself knew caves in the Ukraine where one might knock rock crystals from the walls. But perhaps this had a certain significance.

"You know as well as I," returned Pan Andrew, "that it disappeared on that same night that you attacked my lodgings. If you have it not, I know not where it is to be found."

"It disappeared!" Peter was at first shocked, then incredulous. "You lie!" he shrieked. "You lie! You have it still. I will find a way. . . . Come here!" he called to Michael the Snake. "Take this boy to the house where he lives, and keep always your knife at his throat. I will stay with the old one here, and if you do not return in a quarter of an hour, we will put this Pole out of all trouble in this world. . . . No," he continued, as if changing his mind, "I will go with the brat myself. While we look the house over, you keep your sword close to the old fox's throat. If the boy leads me the wrong way, I'll slit his throat, likewise if he tries to betray me. But if we do not return with the crystal in a reasonable time, do as I have told you."

That Pan Andrew would gladly give up the crystal to save not only his own life but that of a boy, the Cossack had believed firmly. Therefore his denial of the possession of the crystal was unlooked for and baffling. However, he dismissed the matter from his mind promptly. Undoubtedly, Pan Andrew had lied to him, and unless something unforeseen happened, it would be but a matter of a few minutes' time before the crystal was in his own hands. It was true that Joseph might not know the exact hiding place of the crystal; what he did know was that the men in the tower would kill his father if he did not return at once with the prize, and he and the mother would make a quick search of the house in order to find it and redeem the father. It did occur to Peter that perhaps Pan Andrew had deposited it elsewhere, but if the house did not give up its prize, then they would return and try to torture the information out of the father.

"Stay," he said suddenly, just as Joseph's captor delivered the boy into his hands, "the hourglass there on the table shows that the sand has fallen to the second hour. It is time that the trumpet was sounded from this place, otherwise someone may suspect that something is wrong and come up here to see. . . . You, boy—you trumpet sometimes, I know. Surprises you, does it? Peter has eyes and ears everywhere. So, before we set out to get this precious stone, take down that trumpet from the wall. . . . No, leave it there a moment, and come here."

He led him to the bell rope outside and stood over him.

"Ring twice upon the bell; then get your trumpet and play your Heynal from the four windows."

He watched the boy carefully, with his knife gleaming in his hands, as Joseph tugged twice at the cord that moved the hammer against the bell.

"Do as you always do, and play no tricks."

As Joseph went back to the little room and took up the trumpet, he was thinking of another young trumpeter who, standing in the old tower over this same spot, had fallen pierced by an arrow while performing his duty. And it seemed curious that he too was called upon to show his mettle in much the same way. In his heart much of the first tumult of fear had died out. There had come to him that gift of everlasting staunchness which had been one of the most characteristic qualities of the Polish people. It was perhaps the inspiration which the thought of that other trumpeter had brought, for immediately afterward and at the minute that he had thrust the trumpet through the tower opening on the west, his mind flew back to his conversation one day with Elzbietka. He had spoken in jest that day about the Heynal, but she had taken it as a childish secret—bless her!—he was sure that she would remember.

This hope increased instantly. He knew that Elzbietka was awake at the second hour; she had known that it would be at that hour that he would take his father's place, and if the Heynal was played straight through and two or three notes were added at the end where usually the music broke off on the broken note, she would know that something was wrong. What would she do? Her uncle, lost in his experiments, would only laugh at her fancy, as he would call it. Would she dare in the night to go to Jan Kanty? If she did, it was possible that Kanty could summon the watch quickly enough to save his father's life, for he felt in his heart that Peter meant to kill Pan Andrew after the crystal was found.

It all depended on this. Did Peter know the story of the Tartar invasion and the broken note at the end of the Heynal? God must be trusted that he did not. This prayer was on Joseph's lips as Peter said, "Now for your music."

Up went the trumpet.

Then it seemed to Joseph that he had once done this very thing before. The whole world changed beneath him. The great stone city had become wood, and it was everywhere in flames. Men of short stature and ugly faces were riding about furiously on little horses. Close at hand a man had descended from his horse and had drawn a bow from his shoulders and an iron-tipped arrow from a quiver. The bow bent, the arrow was notched.

He played.

Peter nodded. The Heynal was not new to him, and he knew that the boy was playing as usual— that is, he knew up to a central point. Joseph hesitated at the place where the music ordinarily breaks off—this time he added three notes of his own, which definitely finished the Heynal. It took courage to play those notes, for he knew not but at any moment he might feel the Cossack's dagger in his throat. At length, he let the trumpet fall and looked about.

The blood surged into his head with a rush. The Cossack was nodding approval! He did not know, then!

He went to the windows at south, east, and north successively and played as he had already played.

"Now hurry for your lodgings!"

Peter gripped the boy's arm and pushed him ahead all the way down the stairs, after giving final orders to the men who guarded Pan Andrew. They found no one in the square below and slunk along in the shadows toward the university district. The Cossack was exulting again that his plans were working, and as he went along he looked about him for a quiet corner where he could finish Joseph with his dagger once he had the crystal in his hands and was on the way back to the tower. Then they would settle with the father and there would be no one left to give information concerning them. A company of Armenian merchants would leave the city unhindered in the course of the following day.

12

Elzbietka Misses the Broken Note

Very much earlier on this same eventful night a girlish figure emerged from the door leading to Alchemist Kreutz's lodgings, on the third floor of the building where Pan Andrew lived, and stole quietly down the steps to the second floor. Here she rapped three times. In a space of perhaps a minute, the door was thrown back a little, and Joseph's mother peered cautiously out through the crack.

"Come in, child," she said heartily as she recognized Elzbietka's face.

"What brings you out so late?" she inquired a moment later, as she shot the heavy bolts back into place and secured the door. "Has the student Tring been troubling you or your uncle lately, or what is it? Sit there at the table where I was just finishing my sewing for the day and tell me the whole story."

"Yes," answered the girl, "it is the student Tring. He and uncle are in the loft now, and I am somewhat frightened—they have been talking more queerly than ever all this evening."

"You must stay with me here this night," the

woman said. "It's a shame that such a scholar as your uncle should have anything to do with that student, Tring. I fear that young man very much. He seems to me like one who has grown old and then become young again. When he looks at me with those great dark eyes it seems as if he were thinking of terrible things—"

"I will stay here, and gladly, Mother," she answered, for in these months of sweet acquaintanceship the affection of the woman and girl had become much like that which exists between mother and daughter, "but it is not that I fear anything, myself, from the student Tring. It is really my uncle's conduct these few weeks that troubles me, and more especially his conduct since that night when the men came here to steal. He is so changed!"

"I have seen," Joseph's mother replied. "But has he ever been cruel to you?"

"Oh, no! Never that. But he is not at all as he was when we first came here to live. Then he was full of merriment, ready to talk or laugh with me, eager to go somewhere or to see something that would be of pleasure to us both. Now he does not seem to think of me at all. He is always like one in a dream. Sometimes when I speak to him he does not seem to hear. Other times he answers my questions queerly, saying things that I had not thought of. He is caught up in something that I fear, and something that has little good in it."

"It's the student Tring who has done all this."

"Yes, I think that he has done much of it. They two are together every night, and they work together in the loft above my head. I can hear them moving about occasionally, though sometimes a terrible silence is all that there is."

"My dear child," the woman laid her work by for the moment, "this is always your home here. Come here when there is anything to trouble you. . . . The little bed is always yours. . . . We, too, are greatly troubled as well, as perhaps you know. Pan Andrew has not been the same since that accursed night. . . . Yet if one had but sense, we have here all that should make man happy: children, love, bread, and a house—why must men be always sighing and striving for that which they have not?"

"We were so happy before," continued Elzbietka. "It seems to me that the student Tring has some charm over my uncle which he cannot resist."

"Heaven help us," exclaimed the woman, making the sign of the cross. "And have you any idea what is going on in the loft above you?"

"None." The girl shuddered. "It is some terrible thing. Tonight both men spoke in such a peculiar way that I was frightened when they first came together. And ever since that they have been speaking more wildly, I think, than ever before. My uncle keeps saying, 'This will drive me mad,' and Tring says to him again, 'There is nothing of harm in it. Try once more.' Then again there is silence and my uncle speaks shortly, mad things— and I was frightened and came here."

"My poor child."

"Just before I came downstairs Tring was speaking to my uncle as if he were a common servant.

And my uncle instead of being angry seemed to be trying to please the student. At last Tring said: 'This, now, you must do. You must learn the secret which will change brass into gold. Once you have gold, then you have the power to do all that man can do. You can go about over the earth and see all that there is to see, you can study with the most famous masters and buy all that you please.' He repeated over and over again the word 'gold,' and it seemed to me that while he was speaking my uncle was working at something, for he never answered a word."

The woman shook her head. "I have known of those who sought to make gold out of baser metal. But no good ever befell them. . . ." Then thinking that she needed to draw the girl's thoughts away from herself and her troubles, she said, "I am often lonely these nights when Joseph and his father are away. Yet I often listen for the sound of the trumpet in the church tower and I know that everything is well with them."

"And I. Joseph begins at the second hour. We have a secret, he and I, and I always listen for him to play."

"Bless your heart. Do you mean to say that you lie awake until the second hour?"

"I do when he is playing. For he is my best friend, and one should be loyal unto friends."

"Can you tell when he is playing, and when the father?"

"I could easily at first. Now it is much harder, but I think that I could distinguish did I not know at what hours each played. His notes are not quite so pointed as the father's, but they are becoming more and more like them all the time."

The conversation ran to other matters, and it grew late. Finally, the woman made up a bed for the girl on a small couch which Joseph and his father had built. It was close to the outer door, and directly below the casement, over which a piece of tapestry hung; the window was open in this fair weather, and Elzbietka could easily hear noises from outside, especially the sound of the church bells and the trumpet, for the window faced in the direction of the tower. Joseph's mother retired to the second room, where she slept when Joseph was at the church, and Elzbietka, without undressing, for she feared lest the alchemist should call her suddenly, threw herself on the couch and tried to sleep.

She found sleep impossible. Visions of some terrible thing happening to her uncle and the student kept her thoughts boiling like water in a kettle. She kept remembering the words that other people had said, the remarks made by other students, the whispers up and down the lane that Pan Kreutz was engaged in some terrible work of black magic.

It was a superstitious age, an age when people believed that powers of evil could be called upon, like human beings, to perform certain dark deeds —that souls of the dead forever haunted certain lonely places on earth and would answer a question if one but knew how to address them. If a black cat crossed one's path, then bad luck was sure to follow; if an owl hooted at exactly midnight from the tower of some deserted church, then the witches were riding through the air on brooms or branches; if a dog howled in the night, it was a sign that someone living near by was about to die.

There were people who fostered such ideas for their own benefit. They were for the most part necromancers or magicians who took the gold of credulous ones for telling them of their own futures or for warding off some impending evil from them. Perhaps some few of these believed themselves honest; the greater number were thoroughly dishonest and unscrupulous, men who wore dark robes and practiced dark ways simply to frighten superstitious folk into giving them money. These magicians sold articles, called "tokens," which were guaranteed to keep away certain evils. A little ball of black stone would prevent the possessor from being bitten by snakes. The little yellow, glasslike substance created when lightning struck in sand and melted the fine particles was greatly valued; crumbled and taken internally, it would prevent stomach trouble. Worn about the neck in a small bag, it would keep off lightning. Certain little bones from the bodies of cats, dogs, and hares had properties of benefit; the heart of a frog had many mystic qualities.

It was quite apparent in the case of the alchemist Kreutz that something was going on that was undermining his health and perhaps his reason. Such a change as had come over him was not at all normal in a man with such a strong body and mind as he possessed. And as Elzbietka lay awake thinking of one thing after another, she became a prey to many strange fears, among them this one: that

Kreutz was no longer the master of his own soul, that somehow the student Tring had become the master of it; that Tring had discovered something in his studies which he was working out at the expense of the man who naturally should have been his teacher and master.

The trumpet had in the meanwhile sounded the first hour, but still she was not able to sleep. Her natural thoughts of her uncle and Tring were followed by a flood of fanciful imaginings, and in them she saw the figures warped and distorted out of their natural proportions; persons who are sick and persons who carry troubles in their minds experience this frequently, at a time when the body is tired and aching for sleep and yet when the mind is overactive with worries. Her uncle, at one minute of normal and ordinary size, seemed at intervals to shrink or enlarge without warning; Tring was now a student of the collegiate type, now a nightmare of a thing with the head of a pumpkin that grew until the whole sky was filled with the darkness of his shadow. They were engaged in many nefarious enterprises: they were releasing great hordes of bats from baskets, bats that they had created out of old sandals; they were leaping into the air and catching huge birds like eagles, which they were imprisoning under the roof of the loft; they were mixing fiery liquids that hissed and bubbled and foamed—they were doing a thousand things at once and all of them somehow of evil. For nearly an hour these phantoms of half sleep danced in her brain, and then suddenly the bell on the tower sounded twice.

"The second hour," she exclaimed, the drowsy phantoms of her brain taking sudden flight.

The Heynal began. That is Joseph, she thought.

She was humming the tune, already following him note by note—she reached the place where the hymn ended, and ceased there, to wait until he began to play again from the second of the four windows. But the next second she realized to her vast amazement that Joseph had not stopped upon the broken note that came at the end of the Heynal, but had added a note or two and brought the little hymn to an end in the way that pieces of music usually end.

Elzbietka sat upright on the bed, although she was quite certain that some trick had been played upon her by her senses. Perhaps I was but half awake, she thought. I will listen more closely when he plays it the second time.

He began to play from the south side. This time she did not hum the tune over, but followed each note intently. When he had finished she realized that for the second time he had not stopped upon the broken note, but had gone ahead with the additional notes which made the Heynal sound like a finished piece of music and not one that was broken off.

The ending of the Heynal, showing the broken note.

The Heynal as Joseph played it, showing the notes which he added.

"He *is* playing it wrongly," she repeated to herself.

He played next on the east side, but the wind carried the sound away this time. When he came to the last window, the window on the north, the sound came clearly to Elzbietka's ears. "This time I shall know," she said.

At first she thought that he was going to stop upon the broken note, for he hesitated there, but then he went on ahead, as if to say, "I know that I should stop here, but am not stopping," and added the extra notes which finished the strain, just as the young trumpeter would probably have finished it had he not been shot down by the Tartar bowman.

Elzbietka was off the bed and on her feet. . . . He had played it in such fashion deliberately! Joseph was far too good a trumpeter to make the same mistake at least three times.

But what—what—could it mean? That Joseph was in some trouble? But there was the great alarm bell, which once sounded would rouse the town in an incredibly short time. This bell was always employed in times of fire, invasion, defense, and such various events as riots, the visit of a foreign king, the declaration of war—

He certainly would not trifle with such a sacred thing as the **Heynal** for a mere pastime—therefore, why, why, why, **did he** not ring the bell?

There could be but one answer! The girl had half realized it with the very first false note of the first playing of the Heynal. This was a signal to her—to her, Elzbietka Kreutz! Joseph wa**s in some** strange, some unusual kind of distress! He **counted** upon her to remember the little secret that he had made in joking, he counted upon her to understand that he was in trouble. Why, perhaps he was even held by force—here her intuition actually leaped to the truth—perhaps some person was watching him so that he could not ring the bell!

Yes, it was for her ears that he was playing.

And she must act—she must help Joseph—at once—*at once*. Only, what was the wisest course? She could not bring herself to alarm the boy's mother—should she call her uncle? He was still with Johann Tring in the loft—the light was there and there had been no sound of the student descending. Both, she knew, would laugh at her fears and send her back to bed. Therefore she moved quietly from the couch across the floor to the door, where she threw back the bolts and drew the door open. Stepping across the threshold, she closed the door and ascended to her own lodging, where she procured the key to the outer door, and threw a cloak about her head and shoulders. In a very short time she was in the street.

At such an hour as this in the morning, it was dangerous for an unarmed man, and even more for an unarmed woman, to pass through the streets.

Late roisterers were abroad, gamblers, drunkards, thieves, the very filth and scum of the city, were crouching in corners or picking the pockets of some man who had been struck down from behind. The city watch were preventive enough against crime if they responded in numbers large enough to cope with thieves and murderers who often worked in bands, but the law satisfied itself with treating most cruelly the few prisoners that fell into its clutches, and let the great majority of offenders go unmolested. Therefore a man's best friend in dark city streets, particularly at such a late hour as this, was his good sword or cudgel.

Once outside the building wall, Elzbietka breathed a prayer to her patron saint, the good Elizabeth, and observing in the bright light of the moon that the Street of the Pigeons was for the moment empty, kept her back close to the wall and edged her way slowly in the wall's shadow to the cross street at the left, through which she had planned to dart for St. Ann's Street, only a block distant. She was at the very corner and had climbed out from the sheltering buttress of the wall when there came the sound of men's voices from the Street of the Pigeons, directly behind her. Without turning about to see who was there, she darted around the corner into the cross street and broke into a run over its rough cobbles.

Someone, however, had seen her. She heard a voice cry, "Who is there?" and there was the sound of feet pursuing her.

"A woman, as I live," she heard a pursuer say as she dashed ahead. The moon seemed to hang over the very head of the cross street, so that none of the buildings threw a shadow. The pursuers had already turned the corner from the Street of the Pigeons and came flying ahead in great leaps and bounds.

She thought of Tartars and Peter of the Button Face, but it was no such folk as that who followed her. This small company of men was but a band of rags and tatters, beggars and petty thieves and filthy cozeners, seeking only to fleece some passer-by of a few grosz in order to get drinks or a hard corner in which to sleep. A girl of her age was just such prey as these wretched people sought, for they could plunder her without fear of harm, and her clothing or perhaps some bundle that she carried would bring a few coins for their need.

"Stop! Stop! We are friends," the first of them called out. "We would not harm a woman in the street at such an hour. Listen, we will go with you where you are going." But the tone of the voice only made Elzbietka run the harder.

Into St. Ann's Street she turned at length, with the men close behind. Her one hope now was that Jan Kanty would answer his bell quickly, for if she did not slip inside almost immediately, the men following would catch up to her.

However, summons for help from Jan Kanty seldom waited long without an answer. He had been busy all that night with his writings, at which he worked incessantly, when he was not aiding some world-wrecked soul—writings which were to prove of inestimable value to the university and the whole world of culture after his death. Therefore the ringing of the bell took him but a few steps from his work. As he unlocked the door and flung it open, the girl darted by him and into the house.

"It is I, Elzbietka Kreutz," she said. "Good father, I come with news that needs action, I think, and that immediately. But first close the door, since there are some pursuing me."

The scholar closed the door. If he felt astonishment at the sight of a young girl flying through the streets at such an hour, he did not show it. He was, as a matter of fact, used to all kinds of strange happenings. Even when the wretched beggars raced past the door, wondering what had become of their victim, he had an impulse to go out and talk to them and eventually share his purse with them, since he knew that it was only poverty and starvation that drove them to such extremes. But recognizing the girl's distress and her immediate need for him, he closed the door and led the way into his study.

"What has happened, daughter? Has there been a robbery again in the house, or has thine uncle gotten himself into some difficulty? Something of the sort there is, I feel and know."

She recited her story as best she could, for she was short breathed from running and from her anxiety for Joseph. If only he would not smile! If only he would not think that she had been dreaming! But the venerable scholar was far from smiling.

"You are right," he exclaimed spiritedly, almost before she had finished her tale. "There is no time to wait. He is in some grave danger, which may the good God divert from him. Remain here, where you will be safe. I will at once send a servant of the university to call the watch, and will go with them myself to the tower. I fear something of evil has happened."

A few minutes later, thirty men of the city watch, in heavy armor, were marching upon the church. They found first the church watchman securely bound in the churchyard and released him. Then they entered the tower through the unlocked door and began silently and cautiously to climb the stairs.

In the meantime the band of Cossacks high up in the tower above had begun to grow weary of this excursion. At first the idea of an attack in midair, and in a church tower at that, had piqued their curiosity and aroused their thirst for adventure, since such an attack had heretofore been entirely outside their experience. And when, earlier in the evening, Peter had called for the ten volunteers he needed, not one man among them could be induced to remain behind.

But the affair had proved to be of a simplicity that had no appeal for men so bloodthirsty. In truth, so well had Peter's plans been laid, and so secure from intrusion did they feel in this lofty stronghold, and so irksome was the waiting for their leader, that they had succumbed one by one to the drowsiness of the early morning hour, and with the exception of the one man who stood guard over the trumpeter, they were sprawled out idly, or were dozing.

Therefore, men of the city watch, when they had

crept noiselessly to the top, surprised them completely. In truth, they were captives before they were quite on their guard or realized what was happening. Pan Andrew's guard himself did not have time to carry out the leader's command—he was, in fact, made prisoner as he was upon the point of delivering a death blow.

While they were binding the last prisoner's arms, Joseph came running and leaping up the steps and threw himself into his father's embrace.

"Father, Father," he shouted excitedly, "it was Elzbietka who did this." His eyes were shining as he thought about it. "Elzbietka—Elzbietka," he kept repeating. "She heard me sound the trumpet in a different fashion from the way I usually sound it, for tonight I did not stop the Heynal upon the broken note, but played several notes more. She ran through the night alone to Jan Kanty's and he aroused the city watch. I just met him at the foot of the stairs, and he told me the whole story."

"Bless the girl," said the father, tears rising to his eyes. "And you, my son, how did you get free? I feared—"

"The man who was dragging me toward our home heard the watch marching through the street, and when he realized that they were going toward the church he took himself off like lightning into the darkness, without another thought for me. But Elzbietka is at the scholar's dwelling, in the university building, waiting. I must go to her quickly and tell her all, and thank her that we are alive this night."

Pan Andrew was busy with his own thoughts when the watch finally marched away with their prisoners.

The Great Tarnov Crystal! The Great Tarnov Crystal! That was what the Tartar said he had come for. Was it possible that the man had been telling the truth? For what other reason could he have surprised him thus in the tower? For what other reason the hurried expedition into the town with the boy, Joseph, and the instructions he had left with his men? If it had been revenge alone that the man was seeking, then he and Joseph would never have remained alive until now. But if the man had not obtained the crystal on the night of his attack upon his lodgings, then what in the name of heaven and earth had happened to it on that night, and where was the crystal now?

13

The Great Tarnov Crystal

It was late one evening in April, a few weeks after the unsuccessful attack of Peter upon the tower, that the alchemist Kreutz and the student Johann Tring were sitting upon rude stools in the loft above the alchemist's lodging, arguing with much heat some question that had arisen between them. The day had been sultry for early spring, and the sun was setting red over the distant hills, flooding with its crimson the high mound, called the Krakus Mound, over beyond the river on the road to Wieliczka and the salt mines.

Tring sat where he could see the sunshine through the little window, but the alchemist sat within the gathering darkness of the room. Above their heads on the slanting walls, vials and glass tubes of the alchemist's craft gleamed like precious stones, and every now and then some substance lying upon the hot coals of the braziers would hiss up into a little flame and smoke, for all the world like a serpent suddenly raising its slender head and coils above a quiet patch of grass.

"I tell you that I have had enough," the alchemist replied to some remark of the student's. "I am ready to forswear this scientific experiment into which we have so boldly launched and go back to my old studies, which are much better suited to a God-fearing man."

Tring laughed, low but maliciously. "So that is where your courage lies," he answered. "That is the crown of valor that you boast in exploring the wonders of the unknown world. Come," he added after a minute, as if changing his tactics in dealing with this man who was now thoroughly in his power, or so he thought, "come and put a better complexion upon things; we are already past the hardest stretch of the road—if there is to be found the solution to that problem upon which we both have spent so much time, it will be found so much the more readily now because of the sacrifices that we have already made for it. Are the trances tiring you beyond endurance?"

The alchemist let his head sink into his hands. "I am tired—I am tired," was all that he could say.

Tring regarded him with disgust, but held back the angry words which sprang to his lips and expressed himself more gently.

"Then, if there is a fault, it must lie with you, Pan Kreutz," he said. "It is beyond my understanding that such a man as you should find exhaustion in these simple experiments that I have performed. Many another person I have put into trances similar to yours, and for longer periods of time, too, and there has been no harm, nay, nor physical exhaustion from it."

"Alas," the alchemist moaned as if making a confession, "I have been in trances other than those of your making, and almost continually, too."

"What?" Tring leaped to his feet in astonishment. "What do you say? You have been in trances induced by others? Other men share our secrets, then? Who may it be that is also a master of this rare craft? I had thought that no others, save I, in this town were able to bring about such trances." He glared at Kreutz with open hatred and let his fingers stray as well to the handle of a short knife that he carried in his belt, for although he was but a young man, he took his occult powers very seriously. There was as well an element of fear in his emotions, since the civil authorities of that day dealt usually in short and severe fashion with persons brought before magistrates on the charge of indulging in dark or occult practices. Death even was prescribed as punishment for some, although disfiguring, whipping, stocks, and banishment were the most common penalties.

Tring's powers, though mysterious in those days, could be easily explained in ours. The so-called trances into which certain persons have the power to send others we call in these times merely hypnotic sleep. Hypnotism in the days when all men and women were to an extent superstitious was looked upon as one of the very worst works of a malignant devil upon earth. Tring possessed to some extent the ability to summon hypnotic sleep to a willing patient, and the alchemist had become a too willing patient in his endeavor to discover the secret that Tring had made appear so desirable.

And as is the case with most practitioners of hypnotism and their subjects, the hypnotist had gained, little by little, more and more power over his co-worker, until in a few months the alchemist had become merely a tool in the hands of Tring, who, knowing his ability and scholarly accomplishments, did not hesitate to use them for his own ends. He did this, however, with great caution, and enjoined ever upon the alchemist the need for the utmost secrecy, for if it had become known that such tricks were being practiced, the law would make short shrift of both.

"No man," answered the wretched alchemist, "no *man*, but perhaps—devils!"

"Devils?" Tring stood motionless, thunderstruck. Was the alchemist losing his mind?

"Yes, devils. I can stand it no longer." The alchemist rose from his stool and turned upon Tring. "You, who have powers greater than man, know most of what is passing in my soul. The secrets of my craft, the sciences of actions and reactions—all these you know. But I hold from *you* one secret, one great secret which has bowed my shoulders with care and blackened my heart with crime. Come, watch, I will show you something that has powers beyond those of which you dream. See. . . ." His accents became wilder and his voice trembled. He shuffled about the attic as if making preparations for some experiment. He set up a tripod in the very middle of the room and linked the top with chains as if he were to set a bowl upon it; he unlocked a great chest that stood in one corner under the eaves and took from it some object wrapped in black cloth, and this object he placed upon the tripod.

"Now let us have a light," he said.

He shook some powder into a brazier full of coals, which suddenly leaped into flame. As the whole room burst into existence with the illumination, there appeared most prominently in it the tripod which bore the covered mystery. The alchemist whipped the cloth covering away.

It was as if he had uncovered a diamond of the finest water! Upon the brass top of the tripod gleamed in that instant a very miracle of color and light; the object itself was about the size of a man's head. Upon this exquisite thing no artificial effort of man had been expended; it was as nature had fashioned it in the depths of some subterranean grotto where drops of water falling in steady succession for thousands and thousands of years had slowly created it. The outer layers were clear like the water of a mountain spring; as the eye fell farther and farther within the surface, a bluish tint was perceptible, and at the very center there was a coloring of rose. Such was its absolute beauty that whoever looked into its depths seemed to be gazing into a sea without limit.

"In the name of Heaven," shrieked Tring, "what is this?"

The alchemist spoke in a low voice, as one might speak in a church: "The Great Tarnov Crystal."

"The Great Tarnov Crystal!" repeated Tring. "The Great Tarnov Crystal! . . . Why, that is the stone for which alchemists and workers of magic have been searching these hundreds of years. The Great Tarnov Crystal!" He shouted it almost, in high excitement. "Why, man, we have here the greatest scientific treasure of all ages." He began to skip about in transports as the possibilities of the treasure's possession leaped into his mind. "And now I understand," he continued. "Indeed you have been under the hand of a devil if you have been gazing into that thing. Why, do you know that this stone can send a man into a trance in which all manner of truths will be divulged? Do you know that we can learn now for a certainty the very secret that we have been seeking?" And going close to the stone, he gazed into its depth as a thirsty man might gaze into a well of water.

There was this curious property of the Great Tarnov Crystal, and perhaps of all great crystals in the world's history, that it never presented the same vista twice to the man who looked within its depths. Now, this may have been due to many things, to the fact that the lights surrounding it were never twice the same, and also perhaps to this: that the crystal had the strange property of reflecting back to the observer the very thoughts that were tucked away deeply in his head. What drew men to the Tarnov Crystal in the beginning was, of course, its beauty, its color, its light, its constantly changing vistas, and besides these, there was that indefinable fascination that all such stones have. Diamonds, as well, possess this fascinating power to a high degree, though the diamond is, of course, a small stone, and not large enough to hold the concentrated focus of two eyes for a very long time; the crystal by reason of its size possesses this quality according to its fineness.

The Tarnov Crystal was the finest crystal known to the magicians of the Middle Ages. And although magic was frowned upon by scholars and men of science, such as astronomers and alchemists, still there was no distinct line between science and magic, with the result that many of these men found themselves practicing magic when they had intended only to make scientific investigations. It was even so with Pan Kreutz, who ordinarily had but little use for magic or the black arts in any form—until now he had come entirely under the domination of the student Tring, whose enthusiasm had carried him away.

"I tell you that I have had enough," the alchemist repeated now. "I have perjured my soul to obtain this stone, and I am ready to return it to its rightful owners. This stone is a thing of wickedness and blood and it has a woeful history, as old perhaps as the world itself."

"Return it!" shouted Tring. "Return it! Why, Pan Kreutz, listen to my reasoning. I know not how you have come by this thing—I do not ask at present—but you would be scarce the man I took you for did you not use it for the purpose that we need it. After that we may return it—if indeed it has been stolen—or if it sticks within your conscience to retain it now, then perhaps I—"

"Nay, nay, Johann Tring," exclaimed the alchemist emphatically, "to its rightful owners it shall go. Here I have kept the secret to myself, knowing that the knowledge would tempt you—and indeed you would not have known now unless the secret had burned so heavily in my brain."

"As you will," said Tring, humoring the alchemist with his concession, though the purpose in his eyes was of different intent, "but first let us learn from it at once how to transmute baser metals into gold; this I am sure we shall do, then we can be independent of these smirking dogs who rule the universities."

"Then let our experiments be brief," said the alchemist. "I have looked too long upon this glittering thing."

"You should have told me before." Tring again adopted the attitude of a kindly adviser.

"But, in truth," went on the alchemist, "I doubt if we can wring that secret from the crystal. I have now an opinion, though perhaps a wrong one, that the crystal only gives us back our own thoughts. We may not call upon it as upon some friendly spirit to tell us what we do not know—we may not wish and have our wishes fulfilled. I began to doubt it all." Here he rose to his feet and began to stride about the floor. "It is already having a bad influence upon me. I cannot see straightly in the world of men as once I did. When I have looked into it for minutes and minutes my thoughts come back to me crookedly, and while I have taken much interest in such contemplation, I find that there is too deadly a fascination in gazing into those crystal depths. I have, as I said, found much of interest, and were I alone in the world, I might even pursue these studies to the very limits of human thought, but I sometimes feel as if my very soul were getting caught in the rays of that bright thing."

"Might I ask," inquired Tring, unable to restrain his curiosity longer, "how the crystal came into your possession?"

"It was like this"—the alchemist willingly relieved his mind of the secret that he had been bearing alone. "That night when the thieves came here some time ago I entertained them for a bit with some Greek fire and niter."

"Yes?"

"It seems that the crystal was at that time in the possession of the family in the rooms below ours."

"What! The trumpeter and the boy who bear the name Kovalski?"

"Yes, though that is not their name. They are Charnetskis and lived formerly in the Ukraine."

"I see—and the thieves? Tartars and Cossacks who followed them perhaps from the Dnieper country?"

"Yes, the crystal was actually in the hands of the leader when I surprised him with an explosive powder. In the surprise and pain occasioned by my attack he dropped the crystal—the powder blazed about his face and burned his hair—the crystal rolled upon the floor, and I pounced upon it."

"But how had it come into the possession of the Charnetski family?" asked Tring eagerly.

"It was in this fashion. When the Tartars devastated the Polish country in the thirteenth century the village that stood where now is Tarnov was inhabited by the Charnetskis, among others, of course. It was Andrew Charnetski of that day who performed heroic feats in the defense of the city against the Tartars, and to him was presented for safekeeping the great crystal which has come to be known as the Great Tarnov Crystal. It was the chief ornament of the old town, and even kings had come there to see it. For, besides its qualities as a thing of rare value and beauty, it had those reputed properties you have mentioned: that a man who looked into it might there read the secrets of the past and the future; that he might find out the intimate thoughts of other men and women; that he might learn to overcome the elements, to fly through the air like a bird, to walk invisibly, to transmute base metals into gold. In those times no man was allowed to look more than three minutes upon it, for even in three minutes a man might find his head swimming and curious thoughts coming into his brain."

"But how did the Charnetskis save it from the Tartars?"

"They fled with it to the Carpathian Mountains and remained there until Batu the Tartar was forced to return to the land of the Golden Horde. Then, as it passed from eldest son to eldest son, it went to an ancestor of this Andrew Charnetski who settled in the Ukraine after the country had been put under Polish dominion in the days of Vladislas Jagiello. Of course the name Andrew Charnetski is by no means an uncommon one throughout Poland, so little did I think when this man came into the humble lodgings below that he belonged to the Charnetski family which had possession of the Tarnov Crystal."

"Did he tell you his story?"

"Yes. On the day after the crystal disappeared, he made a confidant of me, as one already acquainted with his name and a part of his history."

"But you had heard of the crystal before?"

"What alchemist has not?" he answered. "I knew that it was brought in early days to Egypt from somewhere in the East, and there it stood in a temple for many centuries. When the Romans conquered Egypt, the crystal was taken to Rome. During the years when the Romans were colonizing the lands around the Black Sea a certain Roman officer fell in love with a woman of Transylvania, and being sent there with a legion, stole for her this crystal from a temple in Rome. When his crime was discovered, the emperor sent a detachment of soldiers to bring him back, but he fled to the district which is now Halicz, but which went then under the Roman name Galicia. There he lived with his wife under an assumed name, in a remote village known as Tarnov, and there the crystal remained up to the time that it passed into the hands of the Charnetskis. Around it grew up a sect of sorcerers, magicians, practicers of the black art, astrologers, and alchemists—some sincere, others mere charlatans."

"Surely there have been many attempts to steal the crystal from the Charnetskis?"

"Only one. It seems that men, even alchemists and astrologers, lost for a time the thread of its history, and it was only when a runaway servant of Andrew Charnetski spread the news in the East that it was in his possession that an attempt was made to find it. That attempt, as you know, cost Pan Andrew his house and property in the Ukraine. Who it is that is inciting these robbers I know not, but I have no doubt that the leader of the band was in the pay of some person in high authority."

"Would the robbers taken prisoners say nothing?"

"No, they did not know all, I believe. And like most Tartars they would rather die than betray a secret. Torture could not wring it out of them."

"Does Pan Andrew suspect that you have the crystal?"

"Pan Andrew considers me his friend. And at heart I am ashamed and sick that I have not restored it before now."

"But think. If it had not been for you, the Cossack would have escaped with the crystal and it would have been lost forever."

"I know it. Yet that is no justification for me. I stole it if a thief ever stole anything. When I first saw it that night on the floor of Pan Andrew's lodging I would have exchanged my chance of Heaven for its possession. When I had obtained it, and the attention of the crowd in the court below was turned to the robbers and to the man escaping over the roofs, I brought it here to the loft, under my coat."

"You did well," said Tring, the wildest impulses of excitement leaping within him. "Look—look at the crystal. It glows and dances and quivers like a thing alive, ready to tell its secrets. Quick, draw your chair near to it as you used to draw your chair to me when I was the master of your trances. Gaze deeply into it"—he fixed the hesitating alchemist with his eyes as a serpent might fix a helpless bird—"and now let us try the greatest experiment of all."

The alchemist pulled his chair close to the crystal as he was bid, and fixed his eyes upon it. Tring watched him closely from a distance. One minute —two minutes—three—the alchemist still looked at the crystal, and Tring regarded him as a cat might regard a mouse that it was playing with. Four minutes—five. The alchemist still sat motionless, but his posture in the chair was changing slightly. His arms and neck seemed to be stiffening, his face was taking on the look of an entirely different person; his breath came regularly, but in longer and deeper draughts than was his wont. His eyes became wide open and staring.

"Listen." Tring's tone was sharp, commanding.

"I am listening," the reply came instantly.

Tring trembled with excitement. Not only had the alchemist gone into this trance more quickly than he, Tring, had ever been able to send him, but he was still responsive to the student, who had feared lest the agency of the crystal might render Kreutz unresponsive to him. But Tring had sent him into trances so many times that now his mind seemed to answer the student's bidding automatically.

"Tell me what you see."

"I can see a huge hall like an alchemist's room, filled with braziers and glass instruments. In these instruments fluids of fire are rushing to and fro, and near them are great copper kettles out of which are coming puffs of steam."

"It is the devil's workshop that you are in," said Tring sharply. "Do you see any men at work?"

There was silence a moment as the alchemist's consciousness went roaming through the vast room.

"There is no one here," he said at length.

"Are there any manuscripts there?" demanded Tring.

Silence again. Then—"Yes, on the wall hangs a parchment."

"Take it down."

"It burns my hands."

"Pay no heed to that. Your reward will be greater than your pains."

"It is in my hands."

Tring glanced involuntarily at the hands of the man in the trance. Curiously enough, they seemed to be turning red, as if exposed to a great heat. "Now read what the parchment says."

The alchemist replied slowly, as if reading, and he spoke in the Latin tongue. "HERE MAY ONE FIND THINGS WHICH BE NEITHER GOOD NOR EVIL BUT WHICH ARE SOUGHT OF ALL MEN."

"Good! Now unroll the parchment."

There was another silence. At length the alchemist said, "I have found somewhat."

"Read!"

"Nay, I may not. It is in symbols."

"Then write." Tring deftly slipped a piece of board across his knees and put into his fingers a kind of pen made of wood and a feather; this he had dipped into a pot of ink as thick as paint, and he guided it in the alchemist's hand until it rested upon a piece of fresh white parchment that he laid upon the board.

The alchemist wrote as follows:

"Per $\theta\Delta\delta$ Fit Lapis Philosophorum"[1]

"What else?"

The alchemist wrote:

"*Quod primum incredible, non continuo falsum est; crebo siquidem faciem mendacii veritas retinet.*"[2]

"No. That's nothing. Do you find other formulae?"

"The alchemist looked closely and recited as if reading:

"Thus saith Olimpiodorus of Thebes, Osthanes the Egyptian, Psellos of Byzantium, and Giabr of Arabia: heat the fires upon thy brazier and place thereon a vessel full of yellow sulphur; this thou shalt melt until it gives forth a spirit; when the

[1] Through $\theta\Delta\delta$ the Philosophers' Stone is made.

[2] What at first [seems to be] incredible is not necessarily false since truth very often has the appearance of a lie.

spirit is departed pour slowly upon the sulphur that quicksilver which has its birth in the planet Mercury. In but the twinkling of an eye this will be reduced from its natural state unto a state that is of the earth, black, without life, dead. Then take this lifeless substance and put it in a closed vessel; heat it and it will suddenly take on life again and become a brilliant red."

"Write it, write it," exclaimed Tring. The alchemist wrote. "And is there more?"

"Much. It saith here that this is the secret of the Seven Golden Chapters, of the Emerald Table, and the Pimander. *Natura naturam superat; deinde vero natura naturae congaudet; tandem natura naturam continet.*"[3]

"No more of that. That is vile philosophy," shouted Tring. "Find and write the completion of the Philosophers' Stone, by which we may convert brass into gold."

The alchemist continued:

"Zosimus the Theban directs that this is the true method of turning brass into gold: To the above heated solution of sulphur and mercury add that pure niter which men find in the heart of India. Into this cast brass, and it will in a moment change to gold."

"Quick, to work. Light the braziers and bring out sulphur, quicksilver, and brass," commanded Tring. "Have you any of this Indian niter?"

"I have—a small packet on the third shelf of the closet," answered the alchemist. Tring rushed to

[3] Nature conquers nature; then, indeed, nature delights in nature; finally, nature confines nature.

get it and set all the materials ready for the experiment. Truly and sincerely did he believe that the alchemist had hit upon the solution of the much desired process of changing base metals into gold, and his own lack of knowledge in the realm of the science of alchemy was responsible for the ignorance with which he ordered the alchemist to compound one of the most dangerous chemicals known to man. The alchemist, on his part, was but acting under the hypnotic suggestion of Tring, and had no opportunity to interpose his normal-self sense between the student's intention and its execution. Indeed, the information he had during the trance came from his own fund of learning, although the suggestion of adding niter to the heated compound was but a fancy of a mind grown either tired or weak.

As the student hurried about arranging materials for the experiment, Kreutz sang a Latin hymn which extols the practice of alchemy and the alchemist:

> *Inexhaustum fert thesaurum*
> *Qui de virgis fecit aurum*
> *Gemmas de lapidibus.*[4]

"Compound the Philosophers' Stone," commanded Tring.

The alchemist, still in the trance, arose, and leaned over the brazier. Something flaky and white

[4] He brings forth an inexhaustible treasury
who has made gold from twigs,
gems from ordinary stones.

and inflammable was tucked close to the bottom to act as kindling, and a coal brought from a farther brazier and laid upon this. It turned all black for a minute, then sizzled into an intense heat and ignited the brazier's contents. The flame was at first yellow and creeping, then it changed to blue and leaping. Kreutz put a vessel filled with sulphur into the flames, and sure enough, in a moment the spirit of the sulphur arose in fumes that filled the room.

Both leaned over the brazier eagerly as the alchemist shook mercury over the melted sulphur. As the parchment had decreed, so the reaction followed; in a short time the glittering mercury had mingled with the melted sulphur and become an ugly black substance. Tring handed to Kreutz another vessel, which was closed at the top. Kreutz shook the hot material from the first vessel into the second and put the latter back on the brazier. In all his motions he acted mechanically, as if he were but working out the will of another. He opened this second vessel after a few seconds, and sure enough, the black substance was becoming a lively red.

"The niter; the niter," exclaimed Tring eagerly at his elbow.

The alchemist took the package from his hands and tossed it into the substance now seething with heat. As he did so, as if obeying some unconscious instinct of self-preservation, he leaped back into the middle of the room and drew Tring with him. The exclamation of anger on Tring's lips was cut in half, for at that instant the loft of the house rocked in a terrific explosion!

"Quick, seize the crystal and descend!" screamed Tring, who was already speeding through the doorway, frantically wiping sparks of fire from his clothing.

The exploding substances had sent their flames into the dry roof and walls of the house, and fire was leaping through them merrily. Everything in the room was beginning to blaze, and in two minutes more it would have been impossible to leave. The alchemist, still in a daze, took the crystal as he had been commanded, and made for the stairway. The stone gleamed in his hands like a million diamonds, rubies, and emeralds where the flames fell upon it, and he clutched it with all the strength of his right hand as he clung to the stair rail with his left, now swaying out over the court like a drunken man, now regaining his hold and descending another stair. But the student had been more nimble, and by the time that the alchemist had descended to the third floor of the house, Johann was down the stairs and through the gate, calling with all his might for the watch to notify the water master that the house above him was in flames. No watch was in sight, and so he sought one at full speed, and while he was searching, Pan Kreutz had reached the open door and disappeared in the night, the Great Tarnov Crystal hidden under the folds of his black gown.

But behind him the flames had eaten through the roof of his house and had leaped to the adjoining house. In a few minutes they had bounded clear across an open court nearby, and had laid hold of one of the pensions of the university. The wind, then veering, swept the flames in a seething mass in the direction of the great Rynek, and in less than fifteen minutes after the flight of the two men from the loft of the building, the university section of Krakow was in the grip of a terrible conflagration that threatened to devour the whole city.

14

A Great Fire Rages

Since earliest times Krakow was divided into four sections—the Castle Quarter, the Potters' Quarter, the Butchers' Quarter, and the Slavkov. At the head of each of these districts was a quartermaster, who was responsible for everything that went on in his district, the fighting of fires being one of his chief concerns. Therefore the watchman from one of the streets that lay in the districts threatened by the fire went pounding at the gate of the quartermaster's house, shouting "Fire" at the top of his lungs in order to send the servants flying to the master. In a short time the quartermaster was up and dressed and had sent summons to the water master, who had charge of the town reservoir and aqueducts.

The bell meanwhile began to sound clamorously from the tower of the Church of Our Lady Mary, for the watchman there had caught sight of the flames. Cries of "Fire" were now being echoed from all sections of the city, and in the red glare which was beginning to illumine all the grim

Gothic buildings and churches, a very tumult of confusion was arising. The water master had already set his machinery in motion, and drummers were pounding away at their drums in all the city streets in order to awaken the merchants and their apprentices, upon whom fell the burden of fighting the flames. All the town guilds were assembling, companies of servants from the palaces were filling buckets of water and taking positions on the roofs of their own houses, and all citizens were busily getting down from the wall, hooks and axes and pails such as the law required them to keep for such emergencies.

A fire of any size in Krakow was a serious thing in those days, for there were hundreds upon hundreds of wooden and part-wooden houses clustered together in the thickly populated streets. In the section about the old university the majority of dwellings were very ancient, dry, and cobwebbed everywhere, and a single spark upon their roofs was enough to turn them in exceedingly rapid fashion into belching furnaces of flame and smoke. As the fire raced through these streets, the inhabitants poured out in panic-stricken confusion; each building was literally teeming with life, and the whole scene, viewed from above, would have resembled a huge ant hill suddenly destroyed or burned out by a careful gardener.

Women and children came out rushing and shrieking. Black-robed students dashed through the streets with manuscripts and parchments in their hands; others came carrying glass tubes or astrolabes or metal dividers; frantic domestics ran here and there with no definite refuge in view save only to escape the heat and terror of the ever-spreading flames. The streets were rapidly filling with furniture, clothing, beds, and personal possessions of every variety, hurled out of casements by desperate owners—and some of this material in the streets had already caught fire from the sparks which were descending like rain in a spring thunderstorm, making the lot of the fugitives even more unendurable. Inside some of the courts those who had preserved presence of mind were combating the fire with much vigor; tubs of water and pails were being pressed into action, and burning walls were already being hauled down.

The water master had marshaled a line of water carts which extended from the burning buildings to the aqueduct; these water carts were usually drawn by horses, and some of them were on this night, but there had been difficulty in getting enough horses quickly, and men and boys were harnessed into the shafts. At the aqueduct, men were busy filling the carts with water; as each cart was filled it moved on some little distance to the fire, and there being emptied, swung about into another street and returned to the aqueduct for another filling. The nearest section of the aqueduct was about an eighth of a mile from the point where the fire started.

Forces of men armed with hooks and axes were sent out by the water master to surround the district where the flames were reaching, for the rapid spread of the fire had made it apparent at an early stage that very little could be saved in the university area. These men were under orders to demolish any building that seemed to offer a chance for a further spread of the blaze, whether the fire had already reached it or not. One detachment formed a line in front of the Church of the Franciscans, another on St. Ann's Street, and another on Bracka. All these detachments were forced to retreat, however, as the fire ate its way out of the district where it had started. The Rynek was the scene of a turbulent mob which had struggled from the burning section in the Street of the Pigeons, and every open space was quickly filled with rescued goods. Two families had even taken possession of the platform where the town pillory stood, and children were being put to sleep there by mothers thankful to find a place of rest.

Amid all this uproar, an elderly woman, a boy, a girl, and a dog were fighting their way through the Street of the Pigeons amidst the debris of furniture and personal belongings that had been thrown from windows. They had all been sleeping when the fire broke out, and not having been roused until the flames were all about them, had been able to rescue nothing but themselves and the clothes which they wore. The boy was Joseph, the girl, Elzbietka, and the woman the wife of Pan Andrew. Wolf, cut loose by Joseph, was the most terror-stricken of the group, but he followed after them, submissive and obedient, not knowing exactly what he was expected to do.

Each of them was busy with separate thoughts as they fought their way through the disorder. Joseph was ever figuring the quickest route out of the burning district, and this was no easy task, since the fire was playing so many tricks. It was not marching ahead in a straight wall of flame, but was whirling about, leaping here and there, skipping this house and fastening upon that, advancing, retreating, spreading to the flanks, all with terrific speed and unexpected vivacity. Sometimes the roofs just above the heads of the fugitives would shoot up in flames—passing these with great peril, they would find that the fire was now behind them and rejoice at the breath of air that fell upon them; then, suddenly, without warning the roof of a building just ahead would belch forth smoke and flame as if the fire demon were working invisibly, and this new peril must be passed.

At length they reached the place where the Street of the Pigeons is cut by a cross lane, known today as Wislna Street, but this lane was already full of smoking beams and fallen timbers; escape that way was impossible. There was nothing to do but to push on through the Street of the Pigeons where it curves to meet Bracka.

Elzbietka was wondering most of all about her uncle; there had been no answer to their hurried calls when they left the doomed house, and besides, the loft was glowing in red and purple flames of such intensity that no person alive could have been there at that time. Joseph's mother was thinking of the father, wondering if he had left his post at the church to come to his family's aid, and wondering, too, if they could reach him at the tower before he began to suffer too much from anxiety concerning them.

The houses were a little higher in this portion of the street, and there was therefore more cool air, in the lower reaches. The fire was still whirling along here, but was not taking hold quite so fast as it had done down below, and consequently the fugitives made better progress. The only difficulty was the ever-increasing crowd that now swept in from three directions, making it hard for the three to keep together. Finally, they locked arms and literally fought their way through the crowd. All about them the scenes were heartrending, men and women fleeing with but few possessions from the only homes they had ever known, children lost in the mad scramble who set up shrill cries and tried to keep their feet as the crowd pushed ahead. Sick persons were brought into that raging torrent of humanity, carried on the shoulders of their relatives or perhaps stretched upon cots. Here was one old man who sat astride a young fellow's neck like Anchises on the back of Aeneas, fleeing from the burning city of Ilium.

At length they stood where the fire had not reached, much more fortunate in that than many other people that night. Joseph waited only until they caught their breath, though he, too, felt like throwing himself down upon the ground and resting, and then started forward again through Bracka in the direction of the Rynek. In his heart he hoped that when he had settled Elzbietka and his mother in the tower where his father was on duty, he might come back with the apprentices and help fight the fire, for there is that in a youth which draws him into such fighting. As they went along

Bracka he heard the sound of horses' hoofs from the direction of the Wawel.

"Wait," he said, drawing the women back on a footpath, "here come soldiers from the castle to preserve order."

He spoke truly, for the next moment a great troop of cavalry wearing mail armor and carrying spears rode into Bracka Street from below and began to deploy in lines that marked the district immediately threatened by fire. A few minutes later, foot soldiers and artisans began to appear, and joining with the watch, pulled down buildings at the edge of the fire. Siege machinery was also drawn up into Bracka, and the buildings just outside the reach of the fire began to crumble under its pounding.

This will prevent the spread of the flames, thought Joseph.

They went ahead again toward the church, but while they were still in the Rynek they saw a company of soldiers dragging forward a prisoner whom they had taken in the burning district.

"A thief," said the boy.

"Bless us," exclaimed the mother. "It is not possible that men could be so cruel as to steal from poor folk driven mad with terror."

As the company came near and the torches fell upon the face of the prisoner, Joseph let out a cry of amazement.

"Why, Mother, that is Peter of the Button Face, the leader of the men that attacked our house. That is the man who met us on the first day we were in Krakow. He it was who tried to make us prisoners in the church tower. . . . See how he struggles—but they are holding him tight for all that. And, Mother, it is not the city watch that has taken him. It is the king's own guard. Do you not see the royal crown on their helmets, do you not notice the richness of their clothing? I wonder what it can be about."

Joseph spoke truly. Peter had at last fallen into the hands of guardians of the law, and this time it was the king's own men that held him. It was evident, too, from the way they held him that they thought they had a prize. They did not stop at the Town House, where offenders against municipal law were kept, but marched straight along Castle Street in the direction of the royal castle on Wawel Hill.

At the church they found Pan Andrew in a very sweat of anxiety and fear lest something of harm had befallen them. He caressed them all one after another and then said to Joseph earnestly:

"I want you to remain here and sound the Heynals for the rest of the night. There is much work to be done in the quarter where the fire is, and every man's hand is needed to stay the flames. . . . I see that Pan Kreutz is not with you. He stayed, too, I presume, to work with the rest of the men?"

"Indeed, Father, I know not. We called many times, but his loft was a mass of flames like to a roaring furnace when we were driven down the stairs."

"I must see, then, if I can find aught of him. He has been on a previous occasion our very great benefactor, and it would but suit us ill not to seek at least his body in the ruins. Should he not have perished, as I pray God he has not, then we can offer him shelter here until such time as he can find a roof again."

But when Joseph told him of the capture of Peter, he looked very serious and said that if such people were in the city, then he had better not leave his wife and the young people. On second thought, however, it seemed right for him to go, for the city was now lighted by flames and it would be easy to summon aid if they were attacked.

And so he, with thousands of other valiant men, fought the fire in Krakow that night. They formed in a ring about the conflagration and tore down all the buildings across which it might run. The Collegium Minus was the last building to catch on the side toward the city wall, and then the fighters tore down the houses near the old Jew Gate and stopped the fire there. The flames swept around the other buildings of the university, destroyed one or two, though not all, and were finally halted on the second street above St. Ann's. Sweeping in the other direction, the fire had early in its progress destroyed the monastery and adjoining houses of the Church of the Franciscans, and had crossed over to Castle Street, where it burned flat a whole line of buildings.

On these and the other edges of the district a wide belt of destruction was created by the fighters. This belt the tradesmen, running to and fro with water wagons filled constantly at the aqueduct, wet down and soaked until it was almost a water wall. So furiously had they worked that the main progress of the fire was checked in seven or eight hours, and although certain buildings and ruins smoked and even blazed for several days afterward, yet the great danger passed when this well-soaked belt of destruction was completed.

When Pan Andrew returned to the tower in the full blaze of the morning sun, nearly one third of the city of Krakow lay in ruins. Fortunately, it was not the better portion of the city, and many of the old wooden-built hovels had been there since before the days of Kazimir the Great; that monarch had successfully converted about one half the city of Krakow from wood to stone more than one hundred years before; had he not done so, it is probable that the fire of 1462 might have utterly consumed it.

Elzbietka and Joseph's mother were asleep on the trumpeter's bed, clasped in each other's arms. Joseph sat outside the compartment with the hourglass before him on a beam, gazing out over the smoking ruins of the university quarter.

"Is the city saved?" was the first question he asked his father.

"It is not now in danger," answered Pan Andrew. "But there are many homeless souls in the city this day."

"Did you see the alchemist?"

"I did not. He has disappeared as if he had flown away on the clouds of smoke that covered the city."

"Poor Elzbietka," exclaimed Joseph.

The girl inside the compartment moaned slightly

as her name was spoken, although she was deep in a heavy slumber.

"I wonder if he was caught in the loft?" mused Pan Andrew. "It was in the very center of the burned district."

The answer to his question came with sudden unexpectedness. There was a sound of footsteps on the stairs and Jan Kanty's head appeared from below. The scholar was leading another man by the arm, a man who had been in the fire—his charred clothes and blackened face showed it; around his shoulders and falling to his waist was all that remained of what had once been a black robe. He kept his hands beneath this robe.

"Pan Andrew," whispered Jan Kanty softly, "I have found in the street—Pan Kreutz." And, checking the other's startled exclamation, he explained, "He is not in his right senses. Something has affected his brain. But he has here something of interest to us all."

Pan Andrew turned toward Kreutz—he never would have recognized him had not Jan Kanty identified him; Joseph felt his eyes glued with strange eagerness upon the eerie blackened figure and the mysterious folded hands beneath the robe; it had been a scholar's robe once.

"Ha, ha, ha!" laughed the alchemist suddenly, "up to heaven goes everything in fire, and yet no gold is found anywhere. Johann Tring!" he looked about anxiously. "Where is Johann Tring? He answers me not. He is lost in the flames, the flames that came so red and purple when niter mixed with charcoal. Oho, Johann Tring! Come, Johann Tring, and see what I have carried this whole long night for you."

Throwing back the black robe, he held up the object that he had been concealing there, and at the same moment the sun, streaming in through the little window on the east side, fell full upon that object; fell upon it and made it sparkle like the myriad of dew diamonds shining upon a morning lawn new-mowed; sparkled like the thousand chandeliers in the king's great hall in the palace on the Wawel Hill; sparkled like the rubies and emeralds that gleam in the queen's crown; sparkled like the wondrous thing that it was, all touched by the red rays of the morning sun—the Great Tarnov Crystal!

"Now whence has that come?" shouted Pan Andrew so loudly that the sleepers in the next room awoke. "Where, by all that is good and holy in the world, have you found the gem which has been in my family for years and years, which all my ancestors and I have sworn to guard forever and to surrender to no person except to the king of Poland? How has it come into your hands after it was stolen from me, and my heart was nearly broken? Did you get it perhaps from that ruffian who has been captured by the king's guards? Did you find it perhaps in the ruins of the town? Did you perchance—" The truth suddenly flashed upon him and he was speechless.

"It is an accursed thing," cried out the alchemist suddenly, reeling in Jan Kanty's arms as if he were gone faint. "There is blood upon it, and fire! It has lured princes and kings to their destruction! It has made men's brains mad with lust for want of it! It has caused good men to steal, and evil men to kill. I will have none of it. I will have none of it, I say." He was growing almost boisterous, yet there was something in this attack of madness that had much of reason and determination in it. "I will have no more of it," he repeated, "and no more of Johann Tring."

At that he fell fainting to the floor.

Jan Kanty raised him, and Elzbietka, who had run out from the trumpeter's room, rushed to him and kissed and fondled his blackened hands.

Pan Andrew picked up the Great Tarnov Crystal and held it at arm's length with a smile.

"Now may peace come upon us all," he said, "for I may fulfill the oath that my family has taken and deliver this to the king. While the secret of its hiding place remained with me, I might keep the crystal as long as I chose, but now that the secret is out, there is but one place where it may be guarded safely, and that is in the palace of the king. Pan Kreutz is right. This jewel has already done too much harm in the world."

"Then you may rid yourself of it at once," broke in Jan Kanty. "The king returned to Krakow two days ago, and we may find him at the castle this very morning."

15

King Kazimir Jagiello

Of all the wonders that the capital city of Poland possessed, Joseph knew of none that stirred his imagination more than did this royal castle of the kings upon the Wawel. Impregnable through many sieges its great rock base had stood, brick and stone heaped high above it in a great mass of towers, turrets, and walls. At its very heart, high above the winding Vistula and the town, stood a strangely built round tower, enclosed and protected by the palace wings, where men in prehistoric times worshiped the old nature gods of the Slavs; a place of rest and seclusion where on rare occasions, when townsfolk might visit the castle, Joseph had stood thinking of things that had been in the old days.

He knew well the legend of Krakus, the hero of the Dark Ages who slew a dragon that had once made this hill his habitation. There was a cave, so Joseph heard, that ran from the fortress underground beneath the river, a secret exit in time of siege; here had been the dragon's lair, until the hero overcame him, and from that day men made the Wawel a home from which might be seen climbing into the air spires and belfries. All this Joseph had seen; he had fed his fancies upon every object that graced the bleak, majestic rock, and yet there remained one glory that had never yet met his eyes. That glory was Poland's king.

But this morning, after the fire, when the little company set out from the Church of Our Lady Mary toward the Wawel Hill, Joseph felt his heart leaping strangely in his breast at the thought of the adventure that was to be theirs. To see the king, to have audience before him—it made the blood sing in his ears and tingle in his fingertips.

They took the alchemist with them, on Jan Kanty's advice, although he still seemed like a man in a dream.

"I found him wandering through the fire-swept streets early this morning," said the scholar. "He had been running hither and thither all night long in the most dangerous parts of the city, and how he has escaped death from falling timbers and burning coals is more than I know. . . . The man has something on his mind, something that troubles him hugely, and with it all, he seems to be acting like one in a spell."

"Do you think it well to bring him with us?" asked Pan Andrew, who had doubted from the beginning that there would be any benefit from the man's presence.

"Yes—I have a curious notion," answered the scholar, "that he may be able to help us. We have much to explain to the king, and the man's presence will make our story more credible. And who

knows, perhaps the alchemist himself may get help
—he needs some light thrown into that brain of
his, and since he is harmless, it will do no damage
to take him."

Pan Kreutz's hands and face had been washed
and dried, and most of the fire grime had left him;
the scholar's robe was useless, however, and Pan
Andrew hung a *kontusz*, or long coat, about his
shoulders.

Joseph was there with the three men; Wolf had
been left behind, sleeping upon the floor of the
high tower room. Joseph's mother and Elzbietka
were under the protection of the day watchman
who relieved Pan Andrew at dawn. It was necessary for Pan Andrew and Jan Kanty to assist the
alchemist in walking at times, when his feet would
shuffle curiously, like those of a man walking in his
sleep, but he plodded along bravely, not yet realizing quite clearly what was happening about him,
yet confident that the two men near him were his
friends and were leading him to some good place.

From Castle Street they turned at length up the
long slope leading to the castle on the Wawel. Behind them lay street after street of desolation, of
smoking ruins, of masses of wood still flaming;
amidst these ruins men were still working valor-
ously, tearing down charred beams and hurling in
tons and tons of water from the water wagons,
which were now all drawn by horses. One side of
Castle Street had suffered badly, the houses on the
Street of the Pigeons were entirely destroyed, St.
Ann's Street had but few buildings left, while much
devastation had been done along the Street of the

Bakers, the Street of the Goldsmiths, and the Street of the Jews and Broad Street.

Jan Kanty's company was challenged twice by guards on the way to the palace, but when the soldiers recognized the good father, they were at once passed along without question. It was another proof to Joseph of the esteem in which the man was held; in himself, however, there was not the least indication of pride and ostentation, he was as simple as a child in most matters affecting worldly things, and yet his name was as magic, even in the court of the king. At length they all stood in the little passageway on the Wawel through which one passes to the palace, and here the guard, with spear raised in salute to the scholar, bade the company wait until he went to see if an audience might be had.

The soldier came back quickly. "The king," he said gravely, "will grant any request that may be made by Father Jan Kanty; he only begs that the company wait a few minutes, until a present audience is finished."

They waited perhaps fifteen minutes, until an important-looking functionary in a blue robe came to announce that King Kazimir Jagiello would receive Jan Kanty and his friends.

Out into a wide court they went, following the courtier in blue, up a marble staircase to the left, and along a balcony. Then suddenly a door was flung back and they were in the presence of the king.

To Joseph, remembering it afterward, it all seemed like a dream, it was all so quiet and without ceremony. King Kazimir had chosen to receive them in a small antechamber in which he often met certain persons who were to be received without the usual ceremony of presentation, and Jan Kanty was one of the privileged ones that he met in such fashion.

Joseph and his father dropped upon one knee in front of the king. He was sitting in a high-backed chair without a canopy, which bore at its highest peak a royal crown; this crown was just above the monarch's head, so that at first it seemed as if it were actually upon his head and he were crowned. He wore a huge purple robe which fell clear to the tops of his soft leather sandals; it had a great collar embroidered with silks of many colors and in many patterns; a heavy gold chain held the folds of the collar together, and beneath the collar folds, could be seen a rich vest embroidered with gold. The sleeves of the robe were immense and hung down far below his knees as he sat there; the robe itself was fringed with heavy fur. His head covering was a simple cap of the same color as the robe, flat, soft, and turned up a trifle at each side.

The king himself seemed the picture of comfort and informality; not so his guards. On each side of him stood a guard in plate armor, with stiff metal pieces over the arms, stomach, thighs, and legs. At the waist they wore short, straight swords, ready for action at a second's notice. These two men were as motionless as statues. About the room stood knights in different kinds of armor, some in light chain with long skirtlike coats, some in mail jackets that resembled checkerboards in pattern and extended only from shoulder to thigh, some in heavy armor and metal shoes armed with spurs.

In front of the king were two pages carrying scepters. They, too, stood motionless as he spoke. "What is this?" he asked as Jan Kanty came forward to kiss his hand, which ceremony the king did not allow. "Have we here some poor city dwellers driven forth by last night's fire?"

"Yea," answered Jan Kanty, "that is true, though we come not on business of that sort. We are here upon some matter that may be of deeper interest than one would suppose. These are Pan Andrew and his son Joseph, by family name Charnetski, dwellers of the Ukraine driven forth by violence and come here to have audience with your Majesty."

"So," said the king with quick interest. "Stand, if you please, and tell me the circumstances of your trouble, for it greatly interests me at this present time. I have much news from the Ukraine, and not so pleasant, either. How come you by your misfortunes?"

"If your Majesty please," began Pan Andrew, rising and taking out the crystal from beneath his coat, "I wish to deliver to your Highness the Great Tarnov Crystal."

The sunlight touched it as he held it up, and the room and its splendid company were suddenly agleam with wavy flecks of light, red and orange and blue and yellow; there was a dazzling brilliance to it that struck each eye with almost the force of lightning. The king literally sprang forward to take the wondrous thing from Pan Andrew's hands.

"What a marvel! What a thing of beauty!" he exclaimed, while a very murmur of astonishment ran through the circle of his attendants. "Where in the world is to be found any jewel one-half so miraculous as this?"

"I know not," answered Pan Andrew, "but it has been in the keeping of my family for many years."

"Then why do you deliver it up to me?" demanded the king. "It is worth a quarter at least of all the treasures in this palace."

"That I will explain. My family has held it in trust these two hundred years and more, and we have sworn to guard it until the secret of its hiding place became known, and then, since there would be great danger following such a discovery, to deliver it into the hands of the king."

"Then its hiding place has been discovered? But tell me first the reason for concealing such a wondrous stone."

"That, your Majesty, is a long story, which if your Majesty so desires I will deliver shortly in writing, but I may say briefly that when Tarnov fell before the Tartars these many years ago, the citizens entrusted this crystal to a member of my family. He took oath to guard it zealously, with his life if need be, lest it fall into the hands of people who might abuse its powers, for its beauty hides strange properties which are allied to magic and sorcery and the black arts, and it has been at times a curse, a thing of mystery and a source of evil. When Tarnov was rebuilt, new dwellers came there and the crystal remained in our family."

"How did the secret become known?"

"I had a servant, a Tartar. He was with me for many years. It was my custom to conceal the crystal in the rind of a pumpkin, and many a time this man must have seen me scraping out the inside of a pumpkin and rubbing the shell with oils and gum in order to preserve it. Because he was a simple fellow, I took no pains at any time to conceal my task. But though lacking in wit, it seems that the man was not lacking in curiosity. And his curiosity, I now believe, led him to spy upon me, and eventually he discovered the use to which I put the preserved pumpkin rind. He left me about a year ago, and it was only a few months later that my house was attacked. I am sure that he sold his information to some Tartar chieftain."

"Could he suspect the value of the crystal?"

"That I do not know. I do know, however, that legends concerning this crystal are everywhere to be found among the Tartars and Cossacks. When they are children they are told tales of it, and all of them grow up in the hope that some day they may find it."

"Thou thing of beauty," said the king, gazing at the crystal, "could thou but speak and tell all that men have done to possess thee. Thou cruel, marvelous thing."

Pan Andrew fell upon his knees before the king. "Take this crystal and guard it, your Majesty," he exclaimed with great feeling, the tears already streaming down his face. "It has already done enough harm in the world. In my own family it has been nothing but a burden, a source of endless anxiety and suffering. My father's fathers, years and years ago, even dug a passageway in the earth, through which one might escape with it secretly in case of an attack, and so cleverly was this passage concealed that for years no one but the master of the family has known of its existence.

"In spite of the beauty of this jewel, I hate it from the very bottom of my heart, and I hope that I may never look upon it again. For every ray of light that it reflects, thousands of men have fought and died for its possession; for every color that lurks within its depths, miseries and sufferings have swept over whole nations. I have guarded it faithfully but no more shall I guard it. I am fulfilled of my oath."

The king looked into the crystal fixedly, and then suddenly shuddered, as if he saw something fearful there.

"I shall be before many years an old man," went on Pan Andrew, in a pleading tone, "My home in the Ukraine exists no more. My house is burned, my fields are laid waste, and all because I had this jewel in my possession and men envied me."

He then went on to tell the story of the escape from the Ukraine, the pursuit, the attempted robbery of his house, the attack on the tower, and the persistency and repeated appearances of Peter of the Button Face, whom he had heard of in the Ukraine as Bogdan the Terrible.

"I do not know," he said, "who it might be that sent this man to dog my steps, but my son, Joseph, has told me that your guards have taken this same Peter a prisoner in the streets, and that he is a captive of your men. Let me confront him here, and perhaps I may learn who it was that drove me from the Ukraine."

While he was speaking, the king gradually took his thoughts from off the crystal, and when he mentioned the name Peter, the king grew restless with excitement.

"I have the man," he exclaimed, "and he shall be brought here. My spies in the Ukraine reported recently that a great treachery was afoot and that this man Peter, or Bogdan, was in Poland for the purpose of consummating it. His description was given to my guards, and a reward was offered. Last night he was seen in the district where the fire was raging, and my guards brought him in. I shall have him here directly."

Two spearmen brought him in; as he walked, the chains which hung from his arms and legs clanked on the floor. He did not deign at first to glance at Pan Andrew or any of his party, but simply looked at the king and folded his arms defiantly and with spirit. Whereat the two guards forced him to his knees.

His air of indifference disappeared, however, when his eyes fell upon the Tarnov Crystal, which the king had set down upon the floor before him. He glanced left and right and favored the trumpeter and the alchemist with a look of bitter hatred.

"You are accused of treason against the Commonwealth of Poland," said the king immediately. "Have you any plea to make?"

"Who accuses me?"

"The governors of the Ukraine," answered the king. "And moreover you are charged with other crimes, among them that of persecuting this citizen here before me—you have destroyed his home and fields and attacked him while he was on duty in the church tower. The penalty for any one of these is death."

Peter did not lose his self-assurance for a moment. He realized more quickly than another might that his plea of innocence would soon be broken down. He fell back then quickly upon another means of obtaining his end.

"I would buy my freedom," he asserted.

"What have you that is worth while to me?" asked the king.

"Much. You are threatened in the Ukraine."

The king thought for some minutes. It rather irked him to give this man his life, since he had already done such damage, but on the other hand he might be able to obtain some really valuable information. The whole Ukraine was in some kind of uproar, and even his most trusted spies had not been able to get to the bottom of it. The usual method of obtaining information from prisoners in those days was torture, and in the field of battle it was employed widely, but often in cases of such desperate men as Peter torture led them to confess wildly but seldom with truth. The Cossack was ordinarily a man of his word, and Peter had enough Cossack blood in him to make him pass for a Cossack in the Ukraine and in the East.

"It pleases me to be merciful today," replied the king. "There has been too much suffering at my very gates to make me wish for more. Your death would in no way pay for your crimes, and it is possible that your information might be of service to the commonwealth. I could wrest this information from you by torture, but I prefer an easier way. . . . Now, mark," he cautioned the Cossack, "I know certain facts concerning what you have to tell, I have information from my own men in the Ukraine, and if you utter so much as one word of a falsehood to me, I will have you taken out and hanged by the neck from the tower gate. Do you understand?"

"I understand," answered Peter, turning just a trifle pale at the threat. He was a bold man, he was a desperate man—otherwise he would not have ventured back into Krakow after having been defeated there twice—and he had no fear of death in any form, so long as he was free and able to fight. But now his knees smote together at the thought of hanging, and he resolved that he would keep close to the truth. After all, the whole affair was finished for him. The crystal was in the hands of the king, and he was not likely to part with it easily.

"One thing," he said in a low tone, "one thing, your Majesty, I beg, and that is that you will let none talk of what I say. For if it were known that I had spoken the truth, my life would not be worth —that"—he snapped his fingers. "I have your promise, your Majesty?"

"You have."

"Then hear what I have to say. I am Bogdan, known in the Ukraine as the Terrible. Two years ago in March I was summoned to Moscow by one in authority, who said that a powerful lord had something to say to me. Now, having an open mind always for new activities, I went, although our people have but little love for Muscovites. And there I was taken to one Ivan."

The king interrupted. "You mean—"

"I mean Ivan himself, chief power among the Muscovites, son of that blind one. He has the ambition to unite all lands thereabouts under himself—as emperor, men say."

The king bit his lips and his eyes flashed. "This they have told me," he exclaimed in an angry voice. "I only wanted the confirmation of it that you have given me. Ivan—Ivan—that one who makes friendly proffers to one's face and strikes in treachery when the back is turned." He strode up and down the room for a moment and then turned to the captive again. His tone was as calm as it had been in the beginning. "Proceed," he ordered.

"In this he has partially succeeded, but his ambitions run higher, and he dreams of establishing his power over the people outside the borders, the Ruthenians and Lithuanians. Knowing them to be willingly under Polish domain, however, even the city of Kiev, which fell beneath Tartar rule, he wishes instead to strike a blow at the Poles in the Ukraine. Someone advised that he loose the Tartars against the Poles, and an ambassador was even sent to find out what would induce the khan to send his warriors to fight the Poles. The answer that he made was a curious one."

"And that was—" asked the king.

"This was his answer. He would lead his Tartars

against the Poles in the Ukraine on one condition, and that was that Ivan should deliver into his hands the Great Tarnov Crystal."

At this the whole company started, chief among them Pan Andrew, for none of them had suspected that such great importance was even now attached to the stone.

"How did he know of the crystal?" asked the king.

"Everyone in the East knows of the Great Tarnov Crystal," answered Bogdan. "Every worker of magic, every astrologer, every chief, every prince is desirous of possessing this treasure. For it is said that, in addition to being a jewel of great value, it has this quality also, that one may look into it and there read of the future—one may also find there secrets of great worth, one may see the faces of men long since in their graves. There are many legends and stories of it too, and since the days when it disappeared from Tarnov, when the Tartars conquered western lands, there has been search after search to find it."

The king thought for a few seconds. "Then the khan of Tartars knew that he was asking Ivan for an impossibility when he demanded the crystal? Does that mean that he meant to refuse to go against the Poles?"

"Please—your Majesty—it was no such thing," Bogdan stated emphatically. "A short time ago a servant who had left the services of this man here," he pointed to Pan Andrew, "went to the land of the Tartars and there spread the report about that the crystal was to be had for the taking, that it was hidden in a country house in the Ukraine. You may be sure that this reached the ears of the khan, whose passion for curious jewels is almost a madness, and when I, going from Ivan to Tartary, learned this, then Ivan promised the khan that he would get him the crystal if it could be gotten."

"You were the go-between?"

Bogdan bowed.

"And Ivan sent you to get it from Pan Andrew?"

Bogdan bowed, though not quite so low.

Fire leaped into the king's eyes. "Dog that you are," he said, "less than beast in all things that Christians believe, for this you must destroy a man's house and ruin his fields, yes, and threaten his life, too, if it would serve your purpose. . . . God knows, my kingly duties lie heavily upon me. . . . All that I seek in this, my commonwealth, is peace, peace with my neighbors and happiness for my people. And yet Poland is ever insulted to the point where nothing but war is possible. It is not enough that enemies on the north and west threaten, there must be plots against our happiness on the south and east. Oh, Poland, Poland, when will the day come that thy sons and daughters may enjoy the tranquillity that God has designed for all people? . . . As to you," he turned again to Bogdan, "what further have you to say?"

"Only that I have failed," answered Bogdan miserably. "And only that I know that I shall go free, for there was never yet Jagiello who did not keep his word. Though had it not been for this creature here"—he pointed to the alchemist, who from the rear of the room had been watching the scene through half-shut eyes—"I should have had the crystal long ago."

The king did not reply. "Take him away," he said to a guard.

A captain in armor came forward. "Deliver this Bogdan at sunrise to the guards of the Florian Gate. Tell them to see that he has safe-conduct through to the border, but that his chains are not to be struck off until he reaches the frontier. After that, let happen what will, but if he so much as sets foot again upon Polish soil, he shall be hanged to the nearest tree."

When they had departed, he said to Pan Andrew:

"In this, my right and duty of kingship in the Commonwealth of Poland, I commend you most heartily as a man who has been of great service to his country. It is a most extraordinary and gracious thing that a family such as yours should be so faithful to its word through so many years and be willing to suffer so much for an oath once given. Therefore to you go my whole thanks."

He took the gold chain from his throat. It was a thing of wondrous beauty, of heavy solid links cut out of the purest metal.

"Wear this," he said placing it with his own hands over Pan Andrew's shoulders. "This chain shall ever be to you the token of your faithfulness. I shall see to it that the state makes return to you for the property which you have lost, for in so losing it you have conferred a favor upon us all. Had the crystal been taken by these thieves and delivered to the khan of the Tartars it is probably true that by now the Ukraine had begun to be overrun by Tartars and the armies of Ivan. In due time I shall see to it that a more formal and proper reward is given you."

Here Jan Kanty made a sign that the interview was finished, and the whole company fell upon their knees before the king.

He, too, stooped, but only to pick up the crystal, which had lain upon the floor before him during the entire interview. It seemed to Joseph, glancing up at that moment, that the instant the king's eyes were fixed upon the stone he became suddenly oblivious to everything else that was before him, and stood as one in a dream or trance, gazing into the depths of the fearsomely beautiful thing.

16

The Last of the Great
Tarnov Crystal

Joseph and his father were still kneeling when
there came unexpectedly a certain happening that
changed the whole complexion of the day. It came
from the alchemist.

He had been listening attentively through all the
talk; he had followed back and forth the give-and-
take of conversation, the balancing of argument,
the gestures, the decisions, even though his eyes
had seemed but half open. Just at this final moment he sprang up from his place behind the
others, like a dog leaping for a bone, and snatched
the Tarnov Crystal out of the hands of the king.

Gripping it, he rushed, like one gone wholly
mad, straight for the door, brushing aside a guard
who fell back in astonishment.

"Stop him," cried Jan Kanty, "he will do something desperate."

They might better have tried to stop the wind.
He was through the door and out on the balcony
and down the steps to the court below, where the
guards, though astonished, had yet no pretext for

seizing him, since he was an honored guest, one of the party of Jan Kanty. Through the little entrance to the court he went at top speed, just as the king, the scepter bearers, and the guards, followed by Pan Andrew and Joseph, with Jan Kanty behind, raced along the balcony and shouted to the guards below. These at once set out in pursuit, shouting in turn to guards at the farther gates. But the alchemist was traveling like a hurricane; and passing the men at arms at the very entrance to the castle, he was off down the slope to the meadows below, where he swung to the left and bore toward the spot where the Vistula curves about the base of the Wawel.

Pan Andrew and Joseph continued in pursuit with the guards, but the king, with Jan Kanty, seeing the alchemist's direction, hurried to the extreme end of the fortifications, where one looks down directly to the river. At the very water's-edge the alchemist turned and beckoned to his pursuers to stop, threatening by his motions to throw himself into the current, which at that time of the year was swollen and swift. They paused, helpless, waiting until he chose to speak.

"Listen," he cried, gazing first at the pursuing party that stood not far distant from him on the shore and then directly upward, where Jan Kanty and the king were leaning over the wall.

A curious figure he presented as he stood there for a moment in silence, his garments sadly disordered, his hair twitched hither and thither by the wind, his features working from emotion—the globe of amazing beauty in his hands.

"Listen!" His voice now rose shrill and screaming. "It was I that stole the crystal from Pan Andrew. The first sight of it drove honesty from my head, as it has driven honesty from the heads of many who have seen it. I saw there all that magicians and astrologers of all ages have devoutly wished for. I saw there the means of working out a great name for myself, of becoming famous, of becoming envied over all the world. I was tempted and I fell, but I shall see to it that no more trouble comes from this accursed stone."

He paused, overcome by the effort of so much speaking, but in a second a flood of wild laughter burst from him. "There was the student Tring," he shouted, "yes, Tring—who used to be my student. Because I looked so much into the crystal my mind grew weak, and he knew and I knew. It was he who said that if we but possessed the secret of turning brass into gold, then we should have power without stint, and it was he who first directed me to read in the glass what formula I might find therein for such magic. What did I find there? . . . Only the reflections of my own crazed brain. And at last between us we have done nothing but cause want and misery and suffering all over Krakow. It is because of our madness that half the city is now but a heap of ashes, that men and women and children are homeless and in poverty."

With these words his voice shrank to a wail, and he stood, a pitiful figure, his shoulders drooping, and his face turned toward the ground.

"Cease, man! We are thy friends," shouted the scholar.

"Nay. Such as I have no friends. But"—his shoulders suddenly straightened—"with such jewels as this, that cause strife between man and man, and war between nation and nation—here—now —I make an end!"

Then, raising himself to such a height that for a moment he appeared to be a giant, he swung about and hurled the crystal into the air with all his force.

The sun struck it there as it seemed for a moment to hang between earth and sky like a glittering bubble or a shining planet. Then it fell, fell, fell—until it dropped with a splash into the black, hurried waters of the Vistula River, so that the circles for a moment beat back the waves of the rushing torrent—then all was as before.

Deep silence fell upon the onlookers. There was in the man's act something solemn, something unearthly, something supernatural—his emotion was so great, and the crystal had been such a beauteous thing; and when Jan Kanty said, "Let us pray," the whole company fell upon their knees. When he had finished a simple prayer, they went forward and took up the alchemist where he had fallen, for he had dropped down as if he had been suddenly overcome by a sickness. They carried him back to the tower of the Church of Our Lady Mary, where his niece and Pan Andrew's wife watched over him.

Meanwhile the king called the scholar into conference, and after much parley, and much weighng of pros and cons, it was decided that no attempt should be made to rescue the crystal from the bed of the river. There had been in its history too much of suffering and misfortune to make it a thing at all desirable to possess, in spite of the purity of its beauty.

And should its hiding place become known— should a foreign power again seek to obtain it, what chance had such a power with the king's army and the fortified city of the Wawel forever ready in its defense? Surely never had treasure a safer resting place.

And so, to this day, it has never been disturbed, though in later centuries many men have sought for it, and it rests somewhere in the Vistula River, near the Wawel, where the alchemist Kreutz threw it in the year 1462.

Pan Andrew received from the state enough recompense to rebuild his house in the Ukraine, and he repaired there that same year, taking with him Elzbietka and the alchemist, who was broken in health for a long time as the result of his experiences. When he came to his senses, a few days after he had thrown the crystal into the river, he had returned to his right mind fully, though he had no remembrance of the dark scenes in which he had played a part. The student Tring must have left for his home in Germany directly after the fire, for he was never seen again in Krakow. In later years he gained some fame in his own native village by the practice of magic, in which it was said that he often called upon the devil himself for assistance.

Joseph continued his studies in the university

until he reached his twenty-second year, and then he returned to the Ukraine to manage his father's estates. He was shortly afterward married to Elzbietka, the friend of his boyhood days. . . . And now, since we have come to the happy end of all things in this tale, may we close with the thought that every Pole carries in his mind—with the words that are foremost in the Polish National Hymn:

May God Save Poland

Epilogue:
The Broken Note

It is the year 1926. The Vistula River now no longer turns at the Wawel Hill and plunges straight through the Krakow plain, dividing the city of Kazimierz from the city of Krakow, but instead swings far to the left and surrounds the whole plain, now the new city. The castles and towers and cathedral of the Wawel still rise proudly on the hill, as in former days; St. Andrew's, which has defied fire, siege, and war for eight centuries, raises its head—two towers—above Grodzka Street; the old Cloth Hall, beautified during the Renaissance, still stands in the middle of the central Rynek. And although the glory of former days is departed from the city and kings no longer sit in the castle on the hill, there has come with the years the growth of a new glory, the glory of culture as seen in the university of fourteenth-century origin, in the schools of fine arts and music and handicraft and trade. From all Poland come students to study and to live in this venerable city, which is Gothic in every corner and every gable save where here and there a bit of Romanesque wall or arch has survived the Tartar, or the Cossack, or the Swede.

But the chief glory of the city is the Church of Our Lady Mary. It no longer stands apart, a monument visible from afar as of old—other palaces and buildings have shut it in, and one sees its towers only, until one is close upon it. Then the sudden magnificence leaps upon the visitor. A splendid silence lurking in its high roof descends suddenly, like the thousands of pigeons that thunder down for particles of bread. Beneath one's feet is the old city cemetery; there on the walls are the tablets and shrines; there at the south doorway are the iron collars that once clasped the throats of petty criminals as they stood supplicating the prayers and pennies of the faithful. Inside the church is a veritable miracle of beauty. Above its exquisite wood carvings and choir rises a vaulted roof of sky blue, studded with stars. Images of stone look down from breaks in the Gothic fluting —tablets, banners, altars, shrines—all strike alike upon the sight in amazing beauty.

But listen: is the organ playing? Whence come those notes that float down from above like God's own music from heaven? They come from the towers, for the hour is striking on the bell, and a trumpeter is playing at one of the open tower windows. And that tune? It is the Heynal, the same tune played by a young man so many centuries ago, when the Tartars burned the city—and listen, the trumpeter breaks off his song in the middle of a note. . . . Four times he sounds the Heynal, once at each of the four windows, west, south, east, north.

And many a man or woman or child on hearing that song thinks of the days when the young life was given to country and God and duty. . . . Poland has been through many fires since that time—she has had centuries of war, a century of extinction. But in all that time the Heynal has sounded with each passing hour and men have sworn each year to keep the custom unto the very end of time. Hark, it is sounding now.

May it bring in an epoch of peace to all men!

Notes

The author wishes to acknowledge his indebtedness to the following persons for their services in aiding his research: Professor Roman Dyboski of the English department of the University of Krakow; Director Frederic Papee of the university library, and his assistants, Dr. Sophia Ameisen and Dr. Wojciech Gelecki; Director Adam Chmiel of the Old Archives Building; Miss Helene d'Abancour de Franqueville of the library of the Krakow Academy; Miss Helena Walkowicz, a student in the university, and Madame Sophia Smoluchowska of Krakow.

The aqua phosphorata mentioned on page 131 was a luminous liquid compounded by the alchemist. Phosphorus as we know it today was first made by Brandt in 1699. In 1602, however, Scipio Begatello exploited the qualities of the famous Bologna Stone and its luminous qualities, discovered by Vincenzo Cascariolo about 1595, and there are other suggestions that similar substances were used by earlier alchemists and magicians.

In the *Iuramenta*, or Book of Oaths, in the Old Archives of the City of Krakow may be found the modified oath of the Krakow trumpeters as it existed in the year 1671. It had been enlarged and translated from Latin into Polish. In 1740 the Book of Oaths was rebound in the form in which it now exists. Appended is a translation of the oath.

IURAMENTUM TUBICINIS

"I swear to Almighty God that I will be obedient to their honors the gentlemen of the Krakovian council, and faithful to the whole city in the service which I render with the trumpet, also that I will be diligent scrupulously in keeping watch, to the extent of my duties, to wit: the sounding of the alarm of fire whenever and wherever it appears, in the city, or behind the city, likewise to sound upon the trumpet the hours of the night and day [appointed], and without the permission of his honor the burgomaster I will sound the trumpet at no man's request. I will be clean in all things and watch the fires in the tower. And all this observe which belongs to my duties, so help me God."